I0531491

Baxter is on vacation, or at least, he's supposed to be. Finding dead supernatural creatures put a wrench in that, but as soon as he finds out what's going on, he'll take time off.

Sloan never wanted the responsibilities of being the pack beta, but he can't say no when his brother asks. Now he's in charge of the pack and keeping it safe, which is a problem, since dead vampires have started popping up close to their territory.

Someone is trying to start a war between wolves and vampires, and they might just manage. Even if they don't, vampires and wolves are dropping like flies, killed by a new drug no one knows anything about. The threat the pack is facing is new and more dangerous than anything they've ever had to deal with.

Sloan and Baxter have each other, but will they be enough to save the pack?

The unauthorized reproduction or distribution of this copyrighted work is illegal. Criminal copyright infringement, including infringement without monetary gain, is investigated by the FBI and is punishable by up to 5 years in federal prison and a fine of $250,000.

This book is a work of fiction. Names, characters, places, and incidents either are products of the author's imagination or are used fictitiously. Any resemblance to actual events or locales or persons, living or dead, is entirely coincidental.

Deadly Fangs
Copyright © 2022 Catherine Lievens
ISBN: 978-1-4874-3298-0
Cover art by Angela Waters

All rights reserved. Except for use in any review, the reproduction or utilization of this work in whole or in part in any form by any electronic, mechanical or other means, now known or hereafter invented, is forbidden without the written permission of the publisher.

Published by eXtasy Books Inc

Look for us online at:
www.eXtasybooks.com

DEADLY FANGS
LIFE WITH FANGS 8

BY

CATHERINE LIEVENS

CHAPTER ONE

Baxter jumped, avoiding the chair the hunter he was running after threw back at him. It hit the ground, skittering across the cement. Baxter didn't stop to look where it ended up. He continued running, his focus on the hunter.

The man hadn't paused to check whether he'd hit Baxter. He was still running, aiming for an opening on the other side of the room. Baxter was pretty sure there'd once been a door there, but it was long gone, and the hunter would take advantage of that and throw himself outside before Baxter could catch him.

Baxter pushed on. He needed to be faster, and he was a vampire. It wasn't hard for him to be faster than a human, even one who could one day become a vampire.

He finally reached the hunter. He reached out, grabbed the man's shirt, and pulled. The man yelped as he stumbled, and Baxter let go so he wouldn't fall with him. The man rolled on the hard cement floor, coming to a stop just in front of the opening he'd been gunning for. Baxter quickly reached him, but before he could, something moved in the darkness beyond the opening. He crouched in a defensive position, and his heart would have raced at the sight of what stepped in through the opening if he'd still been alive.

More hunters.

Baxter swallowed. One hunter, two, even three, he could take on his own. Five, though? And that wasn't counting the one on the ground, who was getting to his feet. He wasn't running anymore, and instead, he was grinning as if he'd won the lottery. Baxter supposed that he felt like he had. He didn't have to run from the vampire anymore. He could attack Baxter and do whatever he wanted to him, and his friends would protect him.

But Baxter wasn't without his friends. His team was around here, capturing and arresting hunters, and they'd find him. The problem was that he didn't know how long it would take them to do that.

"Not so cocky anymore, are you?" the hunter Baxter had been pursuing drawled.

Baxter wasn't feeling confident, but he forced himself to look and sound like he was. He arched a brow, hoping he looked amused. "You weren't so cocky either before your friends joined you. What, you can't take me one-on-one?"

The hunter snarled, exposing his human teeth. Baxter wondered if he realized what he was doing and that it was a typical vampire gesture. It certainly made more sense as a vampire than as a human.

"Shut that dirty mouth of yours," the hunter snapped. "I could have taken you even if I'd been alone, but I'm glad we caught one of you." He glanced at his friends, who appeared eager to start whatever they were planning.

Baxter wasn't. He reached for the bud in his ear, hoping he'd manage to call the rest of his team before the hunters attacked, but he didn't have time. The hunter he'd been running after launched himself at him, and Baxter could only defend himself.

It went well until the other hunters decided to throw themselves into the mix. Then Baxter had to avoid too many punches and kicks, and they started hitting their target. A hit to the head made him drop to the ground, but it didn't put him down. He couldn't allow it to, not if he didn't want to die. That was what these hunters would do if they had the opportunity.

Baxter hadn't been a vampire for long compared to some of the vampires he knew, but he had the same training the others had. He wouldn't allow a few hunters to kill him in an abandoned warehouse.

He struggled back to his feet, but a kick in the stomach folded him in half. He was breathing hard and trying to swipe the blood dripping from his mouth when the first hunter crouched next to him. The man grabbed Baxter's hair and pulled his head back, forcing Baxter to look at him.

"Any last wishes?" the hunter asked.

But Baxter could hear what none of the hunters could, and he grinned. "What about your last wishes?"

The man's eyes widened as he understood what was about to happen. He shot to his feet, gesturing at the others to leave, but they were too late. Part of Baxter's team ran in through the opening, and the hunters couldn't do anything but defend themselves.

Baxter stayed where he was, rolling to his back so he'd be marginally more comfortable. He wasn't up to keep fighting, but he kept an eye on his team, just in case. If one of them needed help, he'd do something, even if it killed him.

Baxter needed blood. It would help him heal, and he'd be as good as new for the next mission.

The problem was that he wasn't sure he wanted to go on that mission.

"Baxter?"

Baxter blinked at Oren, who was looking down at him. "Yes?"

"How are you?" Oren asked. He leaned down and offered Baxter his hand.

Baxter took it, relieved to have help to get to his feet. When he looked around, he noticed with satisfaction that his team had subdued the hunters. Two of them were dead, their bodies already starting to cool, but the other three were on their knees, their hands tied behind their backs, hatred in their expressions. The hunter Baxter had been running after was one of them, and when he glared at Baxter, Baxter winked at him.

"Baxter?" Oren asked.

Baxter turned to his team leader. "I'm fine."

Oren didn't look convinced, but he let go. Baxter wobbled, and Oren reached for him again.

"You lost blood," Oren said.

"Maybe I can use one of these guys as a snack." All three hunters tried to move away, but they weren't going anywhere. Baxter grinned at them. "Kidding. I don't like dhampir blood."

"Come on. Let's get you out of here," Oren murmured.

Baxter allowed Oren to lead him away. It took him a moment to remember why their team was here, and when he did, he berated himself for not remembering sooner. "How's the vampire?"

"She'll be fine. A bit banged up, but they didn't do anything that won't heal."

The group of hunters had kidnapped a vampire, no doubt intending to kill her. It wouldn't be the first time that happened, but Baxter's team had been sent in to rescue her. It looked like their mission had been a success, even with the beating Baxter had taken.

"I'm glad," he whispered.

Oren nodded. "All of us are. What were you thinking, going after that hunter on your own?"

Baxter winced, and it wasn't just because of the pain burning through his body. "I shouldn't have."

"Damn right, you shouldn't have. You could have died. What would have happened if we hadn't arrived when we did?"

Baxter's imagination could too easily answer that question. "All of you were busy with the other hunters, and I didn't want that one to escape. I'm pretty sure he's the boss."

"I suspect you're right, which was one more reason not to go after him. You had to know he had something up his sleeve."

"I did, but I didn't think that something would be five other dhampirs."

Oren shook his head. "You have to think before you act. If you don't, you'll end up dead, and that's not something I want to deal with."

It wasn't something Baxter wanted to deal with, either.

He'd always wanted to help people, which was why he'd become an enforcer. He'd thought it was his chance to make a difference, and he supposed it was. He still wanted to protect people, but he wasn't sure that being an enforcer was for him. He'd been struggling with that knowledge for a while now, and while it hadn't stopped him from doing his job, sometimes it made it hard to focus. He knew better than to go off on his own after a hunter. He'd been trained to obey orders, and that was what he should do. Otherwise, one of his team members might get hurt, and he wasn't going to allow that to happen.

"Sit down," Oren said once they were outside. "As soon as the docs are done with the vampire who was kidnapped, they'll take a look at you."

Baxter looked toward the group of vans and cars parked in front of the warehouse. A small female vampire was huddled in the back of one of the vans, a blanket wrapped around her shoulders. There was blood on the side of her face, and her hair was a mess, but beyond that, she seemed to be okay. She was sipping on a stainless-steel bottle, replenishing the blood she'd lost.

Baxter swallowed, suddenly hungry. He wasn't going to demand the healers turn their attention to him. He could wait. Besides, it was his own fault he was in this position.

He was lucky nothing worse had happened, but this forced him to take a good look at what he was doing with his life. He wanted to protect and take care of people, but was being an enforcer the best way to do that?

Sloan was underneath a car when his brother arrived. He knew Kieran could see his legs, but he was still tempted to withdraw them and act as if he wasn't there. These days, when his brother visited, it never meant anything good, not for Sloan.

Sloan sighed. He loved Kieran, and he'd been his brother's first supporter in his quest to take over the alpha position from their father, but that didn't mean he wanted to be involved in what Kieran had to do. Unfortunately for him, Kieran came to him with his doubts and troubles, and Sloan couldn't turn him away.

"Hey," Kieran said.

Sloan resisted the urge to sigh a second time. Instead, he pushed himself away from the car, sitting up once he was clear of it and looking at his brother.

They were a study in contrast. Kieran was wearing a button-down shirt, and his hair was neat. He looked like he'd just come out of a meeting, and maybe he had. He'd been talking to various alphas in the area, introducing himself and explaining that he'd taken his father's place at the head of their pack. He looked tired but good.

On the other hand, Sloan was wearing coveralls, and his hands were caked with grease and dirt. He was pretty sure he'd run his hand through his hair, getting it dirty, too. He needed a shower, and badly.

"Hey," he said as he got to his feet.

"What's wrong with this one?" Kieran asked.

Sloan rolled his eyes. "As if you care. I know you're not

here to make small talk, so just tell me what's going on."

Sloan had always found it easier to be told the bad news right from the start. It wouldn't help to bury his head in the sand or act as if everything was okay. It never did.

Kieran grimaced. "I might be here to spend time with my brother."

"And I might believe that if I didn't know you're too busy."

"I'm never too busy for you."

Those words made Sloan smile. He knew how badly his brother wanted to go back to the life he'd had before, but Kieran couldn't. He was the alpha now, and the pack needed him. He couldn't step back, no matter how much he wished he could. He'd done the right thing, and it had cost him.

That was why Sloan had every intention of staying as far away as he could from any position of responsibility for the pack. The pack might be a small one, but that didn't mean it was without problems, and these days, most of those problems came from Kieran and Sloan's father. He hadn't taken it well when the pack had decided they wanted Kieran to be their alpha, and he was making sure Kieran had a hard time of it.

"These days, you are," Sloan said. He grabbed a rag from the hood of the car and tried cleaning his hands. "And I don't berate you for it. Between your new job and Robin, I'm surprised you have time to sleep, let alone talk to me."

"Well, I'd have more time to do things if I had a beta."

Their father had refused to replace their old beta when the man had died. Sloan suspected he hadn't wanted to give up even one bit of his power. It was ridiculous, and now it meant Kieran was in trouble. After having to obey their father for so long, no one wanted to go against him. It was too obvious, too public, and besides, it gave anyone who took that role too much power.

"You still haven't found anyone?" Sloan asked. His

stomach churned. He'd known something like this would happen. He'd been dreading the moment, and now it had come.

Kieran rubbed his face. He looked tired, and Sloan suspected he wasn't getting enough sleep. Having a beta would help with that, but that didn't mean Sloan could do anything about it.

"Everyone I asked said no. They don't want to go against our father, and I understand that."

"I understand, too, but you need someone."

Kieran peered at Sloan. "You know what I'm about to ask."

Sloan groaned. "And you know what I'm about to answer. I can't be your beta."

"There's no one better than you for that role. I can trust you implicitly, so I won't have to worry about you going behind my back and doing things you shouldn't do. I know it's a lot to ask."

"Yet you're still asking it."

Kieran opened his hands in a surrender gesture. "I don't have a choice. I don't want to do this to you, but I need help, and I'm not getting it. Robin is doing everything he can, but he's still a vampire, and a newcomer at that. There's only so much he can do, and I'm running out of steam. If I want to make this work, I need you to help me."

"I should have known this would happen," Sloan grumbled.

"I should have, too."

"Would it have stopped you from taking Dad's place?"

Sloan knew Kieran felt like being the next alpha was his duty. He was the eldest son of the alpha, and in their pack, that was how things had always gone. Sometimes, the new alpha killed the old one, or at least, that was how things worked when the old alpha didn't want to give up his position. Their father hadn't had to fight to become alpha because his father had died, and in Kieran's situation, he'd just had to talk to all the pack members and ask them what they wanted. He hadn't wanted to do something they weren't okay with, but they'd been more than happy to let Kieran take their father's place.

Even though he came with a vampire alpha mate.

Sloan still wasn't sure how that had happened, but he didn't care. Robin might be a vampire, and Sloan might have had reservations about him initially, but he didn't anymore. Robin was a great person, the perfect guy for Kieran, and he was doing everything he could to be a good alpha mate to a wolf pack.

"No," Kieran murmured. "Someone needed to do something, and I was the only person who could do it."

Sloan groaned. He wanted nothing to do with any of this. Now that their father wasn't alpha anymore, their pack had a chance to live in peace, and Sloan wanted to take advantage of that. He didn't want to be involved in power struggles or to give orders to people who probably resented him for it.

And that was what he'd have to do if he accepted this position. Alphas had always needed help dealing with their pack members, the humans who lived close by, and other packs and shifter groups in the area. It wouldn't be unheard of for some of the packs to take advantage of the fact that the alpha was in a weakened position to strike and take over their territory. Kieran couldn't allow that to happen, and neither could Sloan, no matter how much he didn't want to be involved in this.

He'd known his answer would be *yes* as soon as Kieran had asked, even though he'd put up a fight.

"Fine," Sloan bit out. "I'll do it."

Kieran peered at him. "You don't have to if you really don't want to."

Sloan snorted. "You wouldn't be here if you didn't need

me to do this. You wouldn't be asking me."

"I need help. Robin is doing everything he can, but he hasn't been here long, and he's a vampire. The pack might have accepted him easily enough, but the other packs around here are wary of him. They needed a wolf to talk to, and I can't be everywhere at once. I need you, Sloan."

And like always when his brother needed him, Sloan would be there for him.

Baxter took one last sip of blood, closed the bottle, and put it on the floor next to the couch he was spread out on. He felt better now that the doctors had looked him over and he'd had some blood, but when he tried getting to his feet, Oren glared until he leaned back.

Baxter couldn't help but smile. "I'm fine. I don't have to sit on my ass the rest of the day."

Oren's glare softened. "I just want you to rest. The entire team deserves it, and the reports can wait a few more hours."

Baxter groaned. "You really had to remind me about the reports?"

"You're not getting out of writing one, especially after what happened."

Baxter already knew that, but that was one more reason for him to dislike his job. He hated spending time sitting down, especially when he had to file paperwork.

At least he didn't have to do it right away. He was glad he had a little time to relax, but his thoughts were running, making it impossible for him to let go of the day.

Baxter couldn't stop thinking about everything he'd gone through over the past few years. He remembered being excited at the thought of signing up to be an enforcer. He'd wanted to do his part and help vampires who needed it, and he had, for years. He'd been an enforcer for a few decades, but he'd never loved it. He'd thought things would change when he was assigned to this team eighteen years ago, and while he loved all of them as if they were his siblings, it didn't make him less hesitant about the job. He'd been able to push all his doubts away until now, but he didn't know if he could continue doing so.

The couch next to Baxter dipped, and he turned to find Oren was sitting next to him. He was tempted to grab the bottle he'd set down just to have something to do with his hands. From the way Oren was looking at him, Baxter knew something was up.

"What's going on with you?" Oren asked.

Baxter rubbed the back of his neck. "Nothing. I'm still tired, but I'll be fine." It wasn't the first beating he'd taken, and it wouldn't be the last, not if he continued being an enforcer.

But Oren wasn't convinced. "There's something else. You've been especially distracted lately, and the only thing I can think of that changed is that Robin left the team. Is that what's got you down?"

Baxter licked his lips. "I miss him."

Oren smiled softly. "We all do. He was a great member of the team and a great friend. I understand you miss him, but he wouldn't be happy with you if he found out how distracted you've been on the job. You've also been taking too many risks, and I don't want that to continue."

It would be easy for Baxter to tell Oren everything he'd been feeling about the job, but he didn't want to disappoint him. Oren had taught Baxter everything he knew, and Baxter would feel like he wasn't grateful if he didn't stay.

He should have known better than to think he'd be able to hide anything from Oren. The team leader was still staring, and he continued doing so until Baxter huffed and gave in.

"Fine," he muttered. He looked around to make sure the rest of the team wasn't listening. He didn't want to talk about this with Oren, let alone everyone else. "I'm just not sure doing this is what I want to do with the rest of my life."

Oren frowned. "What do you mean, *this?*"

"All of this. I became an enforcer because I wanted to help people, and that's what I'm doing, but I don't like it. I don't like that we have to fight hunters and deal with the aftermath of what they do to vampires. That woman was lucky today, but we both know not everyone is, and I don't know if I can deal with finding other vampires killed or hurt by the hunters."

Oren didn't look angry. He didn't even look disappointed, which was a relief. But he looked worried, which in turn, made Baxter worry.

"Are you telling me you want to quit?" Oren asked.

Baxter shook his head, then nodded. Then, he shook his head again and chuckled. "I don't know what I want. I just haven't been feeling it lately, and I'm not sure what to do about it. I'm sure that powering through it will be enough, though."

"But I don't want you to power through it. That's what you've been doing, and it hasn't been working. Why don't you take some time off?"

Baxter frowned. "But you need me."

"I need you and every team member, but it doesn't mean we can't do without you for a bit. You need this. It's not just because you were hurt today, but also because your head hasn't been in the game lately. If you don't fix this, you're going to get hurt or get someone else hurt, and I don't want either of those things to happen."

The team was more like a family than a team. Robin had left, but he was still one of them, and he called every day. They also visited him as often as they could, but it was a bit awkward, considering he was now the alpha mate of a wolf pack. Vampires and wolves had never gotten along, and

Baxter wondered how Robin did it. He probably wouldn't if he weren't in love with Kieran, and Baxter could understand that. He could also understand why Robin had wanted to leave the team, but he didn't have to like it.

He didn't.

"Maybe you could visit Robin," Oren said, once again showing he knew what everyone on his team thought.

Baxter wasn't even surprised anymore. "You think he'll want to see me?"

"Well, he's always found you annoying, but I don't see why not. Besides, once I tell him you've been hurt, he'll probably try to mother you the way he's doing with those wolves."

"Can you believe that?"

"I can. I've always known I'd lose some of you eventually. Not everyone is made for this job or to do it for long. That was the case with Robin, and it's the case with you, too. I don't know if your time has come to quit, but if it has, I won't try to stop you. I just don't want you to do something you'll regret. That's why I want you to take some time off and possibly spend it with Robin. You'll be able to see how things are away from the team and that you can have a different life."

"I doubt I'll move in with a pack of wolves like he did even if I quit."

Oren grinned. "You'd be surprised at how different things can be from what you expect or think. Robin didn't expect to become an alpha mate."

Baxter could believe that.

"Think about it," Oren murmured. "If you truly want to quit once you're done with your vacation, I won't try to stop you. I just want you to be sure you're not making a mistake first. Call Robin and ask him if you can visit. He probably needs help with everything that's going on with the pack lately."

"I doubt the wolves will be happy to have another vampire

in their midst."

"They probably won't, but it doesn't mean you shouldn't go. Robin is an alpha mate now, but he's also a vampire. He needs to show the wolves that he won't lie down and take whatever they throw at him and that he's not alone in the world. He has us, and if he calls, we'll answer."

And that was all that mattered in the end. Even if Baxter decided to leave the job, he'd never lose his team, his family. They'd be there for him, and they'd support him whatever he chose to do, just like they had with Robin.

The problem was that Baxter didn't know what he wanted to do. Since he'd become a vampire, he'd also been an enforcer. The thought of an eternity without anything to do made him want to scream, and he didn't even want to think about it. He was going to have to if he decided to quit his job, though.

Sloan rushed through his shower. Kieran and Robin were expecting him for dinner, and he didn't want to make them wait. They were supposed to talk about Sloan's new job as the pack's beta, and while Sloan wasn't looking forward to that, he did want to spend more time with his brother and Robin.

Kieran had changed for the better. He was more assertive now, and since he'd stood up to their father, he seemed steadier, as if he'd finally settled in his own skin. Sloan enjoyed watching him and Robin together, too. He would never have said so when they'd first started dating, but they truly were perfect for each other. Sloan initially had doubts about the vampire, but Robin had made all those doubts vanish.

Even though a lot of pack members didn't trust him, Robin did everything he could for Kieran. Sloan hadn't thought it would be good to have a vampire with the pack, but he could already see the changes in the pack. Most of the older members were wary, but the younger ones had welcomed Robin with open arms. They were the future of the pack, and it was good to see. The changes had been a long time coming, but they wouldn't have happened if Sloan's father had still been in charge. He wasn't anymore, and he never would be again, not as long as Kieran and Sloan had anything to say about it.

That didn't mean he'd stopped trying.

Sloan was worried about that, and he thought about it as he walked to Kieran's house. They'd known their father wouldn't take this well, and he hadn't. He hadn't been able to do anything about it because the pack was behind Kieran, but Sloan wouldn't put it past him to find a way around it. If there was anything his father could do to take back his place as the alpha, he would, and he wouldn't hesitate to push Kieran down as he did so. Hell, knowing him, he'd probably have fun. He'd always disliked Kieran, but now, he positively hated him.

The lights were on when Sloan reached the house. He knocked on the back door, wondering if he should walk in as he had when Kieran had lived alone. It hadn't been a problem then, but now, Sloan might walk in on something he didn't want to see, so he decided to wait.

The door opened. Robin smiled at him, looking hesitant. Sloan understood why, and he made sure to smile back and try to make Robin feel like he was happy to see him.

He was. He might not know Robin well, but he liked the guy, and he could tell Robin would be good for the pack and for Kieran.

"Come in," Robin said as he stepped aside.

"Thank you. How was your day?"

Robin wrinkled his nose. "Strange. I'm still trying to get used to being the alpha mate, even though Kieran and I aren't married."

"You don't need to be married to be the alpha mate. You're Kieran's boyfriend, and the relationship between you is solid. That's all the pack needs to see you as the alpha mate."

Robin closed the door and gestured Sloan toward the table. "Why don't you sit down? Kieran is in the shower, but he'll be out soon."

Sloan accepted, just like he accepted Robin's offer of a drink. He knew better than to drink coffee at this hour of the night, so he settled for a beer.

"What happened?" he asked.

Robin waved his words away. "Nothing I couldn't handle, but I'm not used to people coming to me when they have a problem."

"I suppose it's going to take you a bit of time to wrap your mind around it."

"Especially when you consider we're talking about wolves. What do I know about being a shifter?"

"Well, if you need anything, you can come to me."

Robin grinned. "Kieran told me you agreed to be his beta."

Sloan groaned and rubbed his face. "Against my better judgment. He needs my help, so even though I want nothing to do with that kind of position and power, I had to say yes."

"He's grateful. He needs all the help he can find, especially with your father still around and creating trouble."

"Has Dad talked to you?"

Robin shook his head. "Neither he nor your sister have tried. I saw her today, and she ignored me."

Sloan frowned. "But you're the alpha mate. She knows better."

"If ignoring me means we're not fighting, I'm more than okay with it. Honestly, I already have too many things to focus on to add a fight with your sister to the pile."

Sloan understood that, but it didn't mean he had to like it. Kieran was the alpha, and Robin was the man he loved. That made him the alpha mate, and every pack member should respect him as such, including Sloan's father and his sister. He knew why they didn't, but that didn't make it right. It might even make Kieran and Robin look weak to the eyes of other packs, and that wouldn't be good.

"I'm going to get you a plate," Robin said as he moved toward the stove.

"You don't have to. I can do it or wait for Kieran."

"Don't worry about it. I enjoy cooking, so I do it often."

Sloan blinked. "You were the one to cook tonight?"

"I did. I promise there's no blood in it."

Sloan found himself smiling. "That's not what I was asking. I'm just surprised you cook, since you don't eat the food."

Sloan had spent time with Robin, so he'd seen him drink blood, and it hadn't been as awful as he'd expected. It wasn't like Robin snacked on Kieran at the table with everyone else. He drank from stainless-steel bottles, so no one could see what was in it. He didn't often get his lips dirty, either, so it was easy to ignore the fact that he was a vampire. The way Kieran looked at him with love in his eyes made it easy, too.

By the time Sloan had a plate in front of him, Kieran had arrived. He was wearing jeans and a t-shirt, but his feet were bare, and his hair was damp. He smiled at Sloan and kissed Robin on the forehead before sitting at the table with his plate.

"Sorry about that," he told Sloan.

"I didn't mind. Robin kept me company."

Kieran's gaze softened as he looked at Robin. "I'm glad the two of you are getting along."

"How could we not? He's a great guy, and anyone who can bring you to your knees the way he did is good in my book."

Kieran growled playfully, making Sloan laugh.

It was good to forget about everything else for a bit. They wouldn't be able to do that forever. But for now, they were just brothers having dinner together. Sloan teased Kieran mercilessly, and by the time they were done eating, all three of them were laughing their heads off. Sloan welcomed the feeling that settled in his chest, clinging to it.

This was why he'd agreed to be Kieran's beta. He'd never forgive himself if something happened to his brother and he could have stopped it. Kieran needed him, and Sloan would be there for him.

Even if it meant going against their father and sister.

"We should probably go over what I want you to do as the beta," Kieran said after dinner.

Sloan groaned. "Do we really have to?"

"Unfortunately, yes. I hope that between the three of us, we'll be able to get a better handle on the pack, but with Dad causing trouble, I wouldn't swear on it."

"What has he been doing?"

"As far as I can tell, talking to the older pack members, telling them I can't be trusted because of Robin."

"That's bullshit, and everyone knows it."

Kieran sighed. "I wish everyone did. I don't want to risk fighting inside the pack. We're already vulnerable as it is, with Dad having burned all the bridges with the other packs in the area. I'm working hard on rebuilding them, but it'll take time for everyone to trust us again."

"So keeping an eye on Dad is my first job," Sloan said.

"Please. I could do it myself, but considering what I did, it's probably better I don't."

As far as Sloan was concerned, Kieran hadn't done anything that shouldn't have been done a long time ago. Their father had never been a good alpha, and he shouldn't have been allowed to be in charge for so long. That was the reason the rest of the pack hadn't protested when Kieran had decided he wanted to be alpha and had asked for their support in taking their father's place.

But their father had been in charge for a long time, and he

still held power and authority over some of the pack members, the older ones especially. It was something Sloan and Kieran would have to deal with, and Sloan wasn't looking forward to it.

CHAPTER TWO

Baxter was on vacation. It wasn't something he was used to, and he was a bit lost. Hopefully, Robin would have things for him to do.

He was on his way to the pack after taking almost two weeks to close all the cases he and the team had been working on. Oren had wanted him to leave sooner, but Baxter hadn't wanted to leave unfinished work behind.

He still wasn't a hundred percent sure that spending time there was the best thing for him, but it was too late to go back, and besides, he didn't want to. He was eager to see Robin and spend time away from work, but it wasn't just that. He remembered Sloan from when the team had been there, and he couldn't wait to see him again.

There'd been something between them, although Baxter couldn't put a word to it. He probably shouldn't, anyway. He and Sloan had talked a few times, and Baxter had been interested in the guy, but they were too different. To begin with, Sloan was a wolf, while Baxter was a vampire.

Of course, that didn't have to mean anything. Robin and his boyfriend were proof that wolves and vampires could be together without anyone dying. It wasn't just that Sloan was a wolf, though. He didn't live in the city, and from what Robin had told Baxter when Baxter had called, Sloan was now the beta of their pack. That meant he had responsibilities and that he probably wouldn't have time for Baxter, which made Baxter kind of sad, but he'd get over it. He was going to the pack to rest and think about his future. It would be better not to be distracted by a guy, no matter how hot he was.

And Sloan *was* hot. Baxter had always been attracted to guys who looked a little rough around the edges, and Sloan did. The last time they'd seen each other, his hands had been dirty, and he'd told Baxter he was a mechanic. Baxter had imagined him wearing coveralls, and he'd almost come in his pants. Then, there was everything else.

Sloan was tall, with brown hair and eyes and wide shoulders. He looked like he could pin Baxter down against the bed and have his way with him, and Baxter wanted him to try. He also wanted to feel those strong arms around himself and to have Sloan whisper everything would be okay in his ear.

Baxter huffed. He needed to stop doing this. Everything *would* be all right, whether or not he decided to stay with the enforcers.

He was relieved when pack territory finally came into view. He couldn't wait to get out of the car and take a deep breath of forest air. It had been too long since he was here.

He knew the way from the last time he'd been here, so he went straight to the house Robin now shared with Kieran. He was confused when he got there. He hadn't expected a welcome committee, and he doubted that was what the people gathered in front of the house were there for. He wasn't sure what he should do, but he parked the car and peered out at the group.

Kieran and Robin were in the middle of the group, talking. Robin had noticed Baxter and smiled at him, but it was a tight smile. Something was wrong, and Baxter had landed in the middle of it.

He didn't mind. He was used to dealing with things that had gone wrong. That was an enforcer's entire job. He wasn't sure he'd be able to help Robin in this case since he was dealing with wolves, but he could try.

Baxter got out of the car. All thoughts of relaxing were gone from his mind, and he rushed to the group that stood in front of the house. A few wolves grumbled when they saw him, but most let him pass until he could reach Robin and Kieran.

"Everything okay?" Baxter asked once he got to them.

"Everything is fine. Don't worry," Robin told him.

Baxter could tell that was a lie. He wasn't going to push Robin in front of the others, so he stood next to him, silently letting the people around them know that he wouldn't hesitate to defend his friend if he had to. He hoped he wouldn't, especially since Robin was the alpha mate, but he knew all too well how wary wolves were of vampires. Some of these people might not hesitate to attack, and Baxter would be there to stop them if they did.

"You have to do something," an elderly woman said.

Kieran raised his hands. "Robin and I were headed out. I can't tell you what happened for now because I don't know. You have to give me time to deal with this."

"But you've had time to do that," a man said. "This isn't the first time this has happened. Instead of dealing with it, you've been bringing more vampires to the pack." He sneered at Baxter.

Baxter resisted the urge to snap his fangs at the man. It probably wouldn't help.

"Baxter is a friend of Robin's, and he's here for a vacation. He won't become part of the pack. As for this problem, I'm working on it, but I'm only one man, and I can't work miracles. I realize you probably expected everything to be okay the moment I took my father's place, but you can't even imagine what a mess he made. I'm doing everything I can, and so are Robin and Sloan. Now, if you want me to deal with this, you're going to have to let me pass and see what happened."

There was a subtle hint of authority in Kieran's voice. Baxter was impressed, especially when the wolves in front of Kieran and Robin parted like the Red Sea to allow them to pass. A couple glared, but they didn't try to stop their alpha or Baxter when he went after Kieran and Robin.

He waited until they were far enough away from the group to ask, "What happened?"

Robin sighed. "Another body was found."

Baxter blinked. There were so many wrong things in that short sentence that he didn't know where to start. "*Another* body?"

Kieran grimaced. "I'm sorry. I realize you're here on vacation, but this is already the third victim, and we can't ignore it, not so close to pack territory."

"You could go to town and get a hotel room," Robin suggested. "That way, you won't have to deal with this."

"Is that what you want me to do?"

Robin hesitated. "Oren told me you were thinking about quitting the enforcers. He wants you to spend time away from work to think about it, and dealing with dead bodies probably won't help. I won't say no if you offer to help, though. Kieran and I sorely need it."

It would be easier for Baxter to refuse and accept Robin's offer to go into town. He was tempted to do just that and ignore all of this, but he couldn't. Robin was his friend, and as a friend, it was Baxter's job to help him.

"I'll come with you," he said.

He was happy he'd said that when Robin's shoulders relaxed.

"Thank you. I've been trying to solve this on my own, but I'm used to working with the team, and I haven't made any progress."

"Well, I'm not as good as the entire team, but I can help. Do you want to tell me what happened?"

"We're picking up Sloan and going to the body. It was found about twenty minutes ago. We'd have gone sooner, but you saw the crowd in front of the house."

"They didn't want you to go?"

"They want to know what's happening," Kieran intervened. His jaw was tight, but he still spared a small smile for Baxter. "As you heard, this is the third body found. None of them have been in pack territory, but they were close enough for us to think it has something to do with the pack. The pack members are understandably frightened, and they're looking at me for an answer."

Because he was their alpha. It made sense, but Baxter didn't envy Robin and Kieran for what they had to do. They didn't just have to deal with the dead body, whoever it was. They also had to deal with the entire pack, and that couldn't be easy.

This probably wouldn't be the vacation he'd expected, but he could deal with that. What he couldn't deal with was the thought that his friend was in trouble, which meant he'd do everything he could to help Robin and Kieran.

He just hoped he wouldn't make a mess as he did so.

Sloan met Kieran and Robin just outside of his house. For a moment, he was surprised to see they weren't alone until he remembered Robin had mentioned Baxter coming for a few days. Sloan had been excited to see the vampire again, even though he'd tried not to think too much about it. Now, with this new body, everything was ruined.

"What happened?" he asked as he walked down the porch steps to join his brother and the others.

Kieran rubbed his face. "I don't know anything more than I told you on the phone. Richard was running in the forest, smelled something, and went to investigate. He found the body and ran straight to my house. He got more attention than I wish he had, and the group gathered there. They heard what Richard said, and they all had something to say about it before I even sent him home to dress."

Sloan groaned. This was the worst way for the pack to find out about this third body. "What did Richard say?"

"Nothing much. The body is sitting against a tree, obviously dead. He mentioned something about it being a guy, but he was so excited and overwhelmed that I'm not sure that's the case. We'll see when we get there."

Sloan quietly grunted. "This is already the third one. You think this one overdosed, too?"

Baxter's reddish eyebrows shot up on his forehead, and he vibrated with what had to be the need to ask questions. It would make sense, considering his job.

"There's no way to know," Kieran said. "And there's also no way to know if the other two overdosed or if what we found on their bodies was just a coincidence."

"What did the doctor say when they examined the bodies?" Baxter intervened.

"No one examined the bodies," Robin said.

He looked pissed, and Sloan could remember the argument between him and Kieran when they'd found the first body. He understood where Robin was coming from, and he agreed that having a doctor perform an autopsy and professionals working on this would be for the best. It wasn't like they could call the cops, though.

Because the bodies belonged to supernatural creatures.

Shifters didn't have a council like the vampires did. There was no one to call when they needed help except for local packs, and Kieran hadn't dared do that. He didn't know how they'd react, especially since their relationship wasn't good. That meant they'd had to keep the discovery of the bodies and what had killed them to themselves, and that wasn't helpful when it came to finding out what happened to them.

Sloan supposed it could be overdoses, but it took a lot for supernatural creatures to die that way. It took a lot for any drug to work on them, making the situation even weirder.

They'd been at a loss, and they still were, which wasn't good. The pack was looking at Sloan and Kieran for answers, and they didn't have any.

"I still think we should call the council," Robin muttered.

"They're vampires. Why should they care about our pack?" Kieran asked.

It sounded like they'd had this conversation several times already, and that probably was the case. "One of the victims was a vampire. They'd care about that. I'm sure that if I asked Oren, he'd grab the team and come here."

"What if another team is assigned to this? Not everyone is like you or your team. It would be too easy for another team of vampires to point a finger at us and blame the pack for what's happening. I can't risk that."

"I understand, and I don't want to risk it, either. But we can't ignore this problem, not when this is the third body we've found already. Oren will come. I promise it'll be him."

Sloan hoped so. He couldn't say he trusted many vampires, but he'd met Robin's old team, and they'd been nothing but nice. They were also lethal, and it felt good to know they were on their side. Kieran and Sloan didn't have any idea what they were facing when it came to these overdoses, and having outside help sounded good.

Robin and Kieran seemed to know where they were going, so Sloan followed them.

Sloan groaned when they reached the body. He should have known this wouldn't be easy. He rushed forward, glaring at the trio of shifters looking down at the dead man. "What are you doing here?" he asked.

"We wanted to see if it was true," Eleanor said.

She couldn't seem to move or look away from the body, which Sloan understood.

The pack didn't deal with death. They'd never had a reason

to, not beyond losing pack members to old age. Thankfully, they'd never been attacked, and Sloan hoped that wasn't what was happening here.

He put a hand on Eleanor's arm. "You shouldn't be here. None of you should."

He peered at the other two wolves. Eleanor and a boy were in their human form and naked, standing a few feet from the body. They were young, which probably explained why they'd come. The last was in his wolf form, but the one who wasn't was hovering close to Eleanor as if he wanted to catch her if she fell. Since Sloan knew them, he also knew Anthony was the most responsible of all of them.

"Take those two home," he told the boy. "Kieran and I will come to talk later, but it's best if you don't stay here."

Eleanor wasn't finished, though. "Is it like the other two? Was it a drug overdose?"

"I can't tell you what I don't know. I just got here, but we're keeping the pack as updated as we can, so we'll let you know as soon as possible. Now go. I'm sure your parents will be worried."

Eleanor opened her mouth, maybe to protest, but Anthony caught her arm and pulled gently. Thankfully, she went with him, the third wolf following them. He glanced back, and Sloan narrowed his eyes at him. "Don't think I didn't recognize you, Michael. If you're not careful, I'll have a chat with your parents."

Michael looked horrified and ran after his friends.

Kieran, Robin, and Baxter joined Sloan by the body. Sloan turned his attention to it, too.

"I don't recognize him," he said after a moment.

"Me, neither," Kieran answered. He leaned closer and sniffed. Baxter looked horrified, but that was nothing strange for a wolf.

"Another vampire," Kieran said, looking grim.

"We need to call Oren," Robin said.

"Not yet. I want to try to solve this on my own."

Robin looked like he was ready to tear his hair out. Knowing Kieran, he probably was. Kieran was doing everything he could to be a good alpha, but he was as stubborn as they came. He was probably driving Robin crazy, especially since Robin knew what he was doing when it came to investigations.

"I don't think you can," Robin murmured. "This is too big for the pack, especially since you're a new alpha. Please, trust me. Oren won't blame the pack. He's not like that."

"What about the others? It's not just him we have to think about. There are other vampires involved, and they might blame the pack."

"They won't. They're my friends, and they'll believe me when I tell them you have nothing to do with it."

"What if they don't? I can't afford for the pack to be in trouble, not when I just became the alpha."

"But don't you see? The pack is *already* in trouble."

Robin crouched next to the body. He touched it as if it was nothing strange, making Sloan shiver in horror. He'd dealt with the other two bodies because he'd had to, but he wished he hadn't had to touch them. He'd been able to smell them for days afterward, no matter how many showers he'd taken. For Robin and Baxter, though, this was nothing new. They looked comfortable as both of them examined the body. Baxter went so far as to pat the guy's pockets, which was the only reason they found the little plastic bag.

"What's this?" Baxter asked, holding it up.

Everyone leaned closer to take a look as Robin took it. "Drugs," Robin said. "We found these on the other two bodies, too."

Baxter arched a brow and nodded. "You think it has something to do with their deaths?"

Robin gestured at the dead man's face. "Look at him."

Sloan did. A white substance was crusted around the dead man's lips. Maybe foam? The man's eyes were open and bloodshot, as if he hadn't been sleeping. That was probably the case.

"It might be a coincidence," Baxter said.

Robin glared at him. "Not you, too. There's no way this is a coincidence. This guy is a vampire." Robin leaned closer and peeled away the dead man's upper lip from his teeth. Sure enough, fangs peeked out.

Robin let go. "The first body we found was a vampire, the second a shifter, not part of this pack. This one is a vampire again. Something is going on, Baxter. Supernatural creatures are dying, and they're dying close enough to pack territory that it's a problem."

Baxter was on Robin's side. Who better to deal with this than their team? But he also understood why Kieran didn't want more vampires around. He trusted Robin, and hopefully, Baxter, but while the rest of the team had helped when the griffins had been around, Kieran didn't have a reason to trust them. Besides, he'd only just become alpha. It made sense that he didn't want his pack members to believe he was too weak to solve this on his own.

But sometimes, things couldn't be solved without help, and Baxter suspected this was one of those times. Whatever was happening, there were already three victims, two of them vampires. The council would be involved sooner rather than later, and it wouldn't look good if Kieran hadn't been the one to contact them, especially considering who he was dating.

But for now, this wasn't vampire business. Baxter wasn't going to go behind Kieran's back and tell Oren what was happening. He'd give Kieran a bit more time, but he wanted Kieran to understand that he couldn't give him forever.

"The council will need to be informed eventually," he said.

"I can't have them come here," Kieran answered. He looked worried rather than angry. "I trust you, but my pack members are different. Besides, there's no way to know if your team will be sent rather than another one, and I don't think I can deal with new vampires. The pack certainly can't."

"But even if the council sends another team, you won't be facing them alone," Baxter pointed out.

"You'd side with us against whatever team the council sends?" Sloan asked.

Baxter hesitated. "I suppose it depends. I don't think your pack is involved, and I certainly don't think you or your brother are. If the victims had all been shifters, I wouldn't think of calling the council. There are two dead vampires, though, and if someone finds out you didn't contact the council, they'll use that against you. It'll make the war between vampires and shifters worse, and no one can afford for that to happen."

Sloan rubbed his face. "Can you give us a little time?"

"I doubt you'll be able to solve this on your own, but yes. I'm here on vacation, and I don't have to call the council right away. Just keep in mind that we'll have to eventually."

"And we can't call the cops, so there's no way for us to know if these victims died from an overdose or what's in the drugs."

Baxter wiggled his fingers at Robin, who dropped the small bag with the pills in his hand. He raised it to take a better look at it, frowning. "Are those fangs?" he asked.

Sloan moved closer, so close that Baxter could smell him. He'd showered recently, and Baxter could smell his soap, but also a hint of grease, probably from the cars Sloan spent the day working on. Under all of that, there was the scent of Sloan, and it made Baxter want to curl into his arms and never leave.

"Do you think this is a drug aimed at vampires?" Sloan asked.

"There's no way to know. I suppose it could be, considering the fangs on the pills, but it could also be a coincidence."

Sloan snorted and moved back. "Do you really believe that?"

"What I believe doesn't matter. The only thing that does is what we have in front of us, and for now, we can't tell for sure if this drug was aimed at vampires. Besides, even if it had been, it doesn't mean it's not dangerous to shifters."

"It obviously is since the shifter who took it died."

"But so did the two vampires. Maybe they took too much?"

Unfortunately, there was no way for anyone to know. They couldn't have tests done on the bodies without involving someone else. That was one of the reasons Baxter wanted to call the council, but he'd given his word he wouldn't, and he wouldn't break it.

"What now?" he asked.

"Sloan, can you call someone to bury the body? Have them put it with the other two."

Sloan nodded. "I'll make sure to leave a mark so the bodies can be found if we need them again."

Baxter and Robin spent a few more minutes gathering evidence from the body, but there wasn't much. This guy didn't even have ID, which would make it pretty much impossible to identify him, even though he was a vampire. New vampires were created every day, and not all of them contacted the council to let them know. Of the older vampires, a lot had never liked the idea of a council governing them, and they avoided it at all costs.

"Let's go home," Kieran said.

Baxter followed the three, thinking about what had just happened. So far, they had a lot of questions and zero answers. He didn't want to assume, but he suspected drugs had caused the deaths. There were fangs on the tiny pills, which might mean the drugs were aimed at vampires. Why had this vampire died, then? Had he simply taken too much, or was there something more sinister about it?

They wouldn't know until the pills were analyzed, and for now, it didn't look like it would happen.

Baxter had left his car in front of the house. He quickly grabbed his bag, relieved to see no one was hanging around anymore, and went inside with the other three. He dropped his bag in the entrance and followed them to the living room, glad to be able to sit down. This wasn't how he'd imagined his first day of vacation would go, but looking around the room at the worried faces, he couldn't say he minded. Robin needed him, and he was more than happy to give him all the help he could.

Robin tapped his fingertips on his thigh. He looked at home on the couch with Kieran, and Baxter supposed he was. "All right, so we have two vampires and one shifter. The drugs seem to be aimed at vampires, so why did that shifter have them on him? Did he take it, or did he die in a different way?"

"And if this drug is aimed at vampires, why are two of them dead because of it?" Baxter added.

They looked at each other. Baxter didn't have answers to give Robin, even though he wished he did.

Kieran sighed. "If we're going to spend the rest of the afternoon talking about this, I need food."

"I'll help you put something together for you and Sloan," Robin said, following Kieran out of the room.

Baxter suspected he went along more to be with Kieran than because Kieran needed help. Robin and Baxter wouldn't eat, so there wasn't a lot to get ready.

"This is ruining your vacation, isn't it?" Sloan asked.

He'd sat in an armchair by the door, and he, too, looked at

home. It was obvious he spent a lot of time with his brother. The thought made Baxter think of his own brothers, but he couldn't allow himself to continue. It hurt too much that he'd had to leave them behind, and he didn't want to think about it.

"It's not what I expected, but I'll deal with it," he told Sloan.

"You don't have to."

"What do you mean?"

"This is pack business, and it's our problem. You don't have to be involved if you don't want to."

"But I'm here. What am I supposed to do? Ignore the fact that you found three bodies, one when I was present?"

"Just don't feel like you have to help us. That's not why you're here."

"I'm aware of that. I'm here to spend time with Robin. But my friend needs my help, and I'm giving it to him."

"Is that why you agreed not to call your council yet?"

"It's one of the reasons."

"What are the others?"

"Kieran asked me not to call. He opened his home to me, and I'm not going to thank him by going against his wishes, not when there's another solution." Baxter hoped things would continue that way, but he couldn't make promises, and he didn't like that.

Baxter was a mystery. Sloan understood why Robin wasn't calling the council, but why wasn't Baxter? No matter what he said about being Robin's friend, he was an enforcer. He'd be in trouble if someone found out he'd known about this and hadn't contacted them right away. Surely he knew that.

Baxter didn't seem to have a problem with shifters, which puzzled Sloan. All his life, every shifter had distrusted vampires, and every vampire had hated shifters. That was how the world worked, or at least, it was how he and his siblings had been taught it worked. Then Kieran had fallen in love with Robin, and Sloan had started to see there was no such thing as all vampires being evil. Most of them didn't even have a say in the fact that they'd been turned.

"It doesn't bother you that your friend is dating a shifter?" he asked. "Or that he's leading a shifter pack?"

Baxter blinked. "Why should it?"

"Well, you're a vampire, and we're shifters."

"I'm very much aware of that. You're referring to the fact that vampires and shifters have always tried to kill each other?"

"I am."

"I don't see things that way. As far as I'm concerned, that was the past. I wasn't turned long ago, and I never understood that kind of war. Vampires and shifters aren't monoliths. I'm sure some of them hate each other for good reasons, but most vampires just want to live in peace. I'm sure the same goes for shifters."

"It does. But we're taught vampires will kill us on sight if we don't attack them first."

"Just like vampires are taught to kill as many shifters as they can before shifters kill us. It's what we've always been told, but it doesn't mean it's how things should go."

And Sloan was starting to realize that. Spending time with Robin had shown him that vampires weren't inherently evil. Robin was doing everything he could to fit in with the pack, be a good alpha mate, and, even more importantly, be a good boyfriend to Kieran. Sloan wouldn't have believed it if he hadn't seen it, but he had, and he was glad his brother had found Robin. Robin's presence in his life had made Sloan rethink what he'd always been told about vampires, and Baxter was, too.

There was also the fact that Sloan was attracted to Baxter.

He'd never had a thing for redheads, but Baxter was different. He was almost as tall as Sloan, but where Sloan was muscled because of the work he did every day, Baxter was lean. That didn't mean he wasn't strong. He was an enforcer, which meant he had training and could probably put Sloan on his ass with barely a thought. But his long limbs and clumsiness made him appear young, even though he was probably older than Sloan. His brown eyes were warm and worried at the moment, and the freckles on his pale skin made Sloan want to lean closer.

He stayed where he was.

He didn't think Kieran would have a problem if he started something with Baxter, but Baxter wasn't here to stay. He was visiting, and once his vacation was over, he was going back to the city. Sloan didn't want a one-night stand or a fling. He'd had enough of those in the past, and they'd lost their appeal. Now he wanted what Kieran and Robin had—someone to wake up with every morning and to go to bed with at night. Someone to share meals, even when those meals were odd because one of them drank blood. Someone to stand by his side, always and forever.

"Robin told me you became your brother's beta since the last time we saw each other," Baxter said.

Sloan groaned. "Please don't remind me of that."

"Why not? Didn't you want to help your brother?"

"I always want to help my brother, which is the only reason I agreed to it. I never wanted this kind of authority in the pack, and I wish I didn't have to deal with the pack's problems."

"Especially this new one, I bet."

"I have no idea how to deal with it. I'm terrified these drugs will find their way to the pack, and while we don't have many younger members, I can too easily imagine some of them wanting to try it just for the fun of it. So far, the bodies we found all belonged to strangers, but what's going to happen the day they don't? I don't want to have to tell someone their son or daughter is dead, especially not when I should have protected them."

"Maybe it won't happen."

"Maybe, maybe not. The only way to make sure it doesn't is to deal with this, but how? I don't know where to start, which is one more reason Kieran should have chosen someone with more experience."

"You're not facing this alone."

Sloan sucked in a breath. The fact that they weren't was the only reason he hadn't freaked out yet. "We're not, but it doesn't mean it'll be enough. I should never have accepted this role, but Kieran needed me, and I couldn't say no to him." He rubbed his face. "Sorry. I shouldn't have dumped all of this on your shoulders."

"I don't mind. I'm glad you feel comfortable enough with me to want to tell me these things, and even though I don't fully understand where you're coming from, I know a bit about doing things you don't want to do because it's the right thing to do."

Sloan frowned and looked at Baxter. "You do?"

"It's one of the reasons I'm here. I'm not sure I want to continue being an enforcer, and Oren wanted me to take time off to think about it before making any decisions. I thought that I could take care of people and protect them by being an enforcer, and I can, but I don't feel it's the way I want to go."

"What would you do if you weren't an enforcer?"

Baxter shrugged. "I have no idea. It's why I'm here—to find out."

"But three dead bodies have thrown those plans into disarray."

"It's always like that. When I have something important to do, someone finds a body, or someone gets kidnapped. It's nothing I'm not used to dealing with, so don't worry about me."

But for some reason, Sloan *was* worried. He wanted Baxter to be able to do what he wanted with his life without thinking about the safety of other people. Baxter should do what he wanted because he wanted it. Hopefully, he'd figure out what his future would be like soon, but to make that happen, they'd have to deal with these drugs and the bodies first.

Sloan groaned. "This is such a mess."

Baxter laughed. "Death is always messy, even when it's straightforward. I think you and Kieran are doing a good job, though."

"I don't feel like I am. My brother needed my help, but I'm not doing anything he can't do on his own."

"Maybe more than your help, he needed someone he trusts entirely by his side to get him through this."

"That's why he has Robin."

"He does, but maybe Robin wasn't enough. He and Kieran love each other, but Robin is a vampire. No matter how hard he tries, he'll never be a shifter, and I don't think he can ever fully understand you guys. It's good to have different points of view, but I'm sure Kieran is glad you agreed to help him, even though you're not so happy about it."

Sloan wished he could go back and tell Kieran no, but he knew that even if he had the possibility of doing that, he wouldn't have.

Baxter was right. Sloan might not like it, but Kieran needed people he trusted by his side. He had Robin, who was dealing with all of this as well as he could, but Robin hadn't grown up here. Sloan, on the other hand, had. He knew every single pack member. He knew that their father was planning something and that their sister was probably helping him. He knew which pack members would be on their father's side when he finally struck and who would support Kieran.

He wasn't going anywhere.

CHAPTER THREE

Baxter had promised he wouldn't tell Oren what was happening, but it didn't mean he couldn't do anything. He'd texted his team leader, asking if he'd heard anything about a new drug going around. He was ready to bet the pack wasn't the only shifter group dealing with it, and if that was the case, he wanted to know. They should deal with this problem differently if it was a pack-specific problem rather than something spreading.

When his phone rang with Oren's name on the screen, he grabbed it and headed outside. He was staying with Robin and Kieran, but he'd barely seen either of them since he'd arrived almost a week ago. He was sorry about that, but he also understood. He wouldn't push them to take time off to be with him. He wasn't a child who needed his hand held, especially not considering the situation.

"Hello?" he answered, leaning against the porch railing, his back to the forest.

"Baxter. How are you doing?"

"I'm fine. It's strange not to have to go to work every day, but I can't say it's unpleasant."

Oren chuckled. "Most vampires take a period of time early when they get turned to just not do anything."

Baxter blinked. "Why?"

"Because for the first time in your life, you're not *expected* to do anything. You're no longer part of the human world, so you don't have to go to work or anything like that. As long as you have a home, it's really easy for a vampire to survive without working. But you didn't do that, did you?"

This wasn't what Baxter had expected to talk about, and while he was curious to find out what Oren had to say about the drugs, he didn't mind answering. "I contacted the council as soon as I found out about them right after I was turned."

"So you've been training most of your vampire life. Maybe it *was* time for you to take a vacation."

"About that vacation. Have you found anything about those drugs?"

Oren sighed. "Unfortunately for Robin and Kieran, I have. It started in small towns like with them, but it's quickly spreading, and we've had a few cases in the city this week."

"Has anyone survived?"

"We found the drug on two bodies, so in those cases, no. I'm sure some supernatural creatures took them and are fine, but I'm worried."

So was Baxter. "Where's this drug coming from?"

"I suspect the hunters are behind this."

That wasn't what Baxter had expected. "Why?"

"Because from what Caley said, these drugs seem to be engineered to actively hurt the supernatural creatures who take them, both vampires and shifters."

"Hunters usually only focus on vampires."

"But what would be the best way to get rid of as many vampires as they can without getting their hands dirty?"

The bottom of Baxter's stomach felt like it dropped. "Create a war between them. Watch them kill each other. The hunters wouldn't even have to lift a finger."

"Exactly. You didn't explain why you asked me about the drugs, but considering where you are, I can guess that Kieran and Robin have been having trouble with it. It's not good."

Baxter agreed. He and the others needed to tell Oren what was happening, but he couldn't do that without first talking to Kieran and Robin. "I'll talk to them."

"Please do. Tell Robin that if he needs anything, we'll be the first to come. He's still family, even though he's not part of our team anymore."

"What's the council doing about the drugs?"

"They've been assigning teams to the different areas of the country where the drugs have popped up. We're actually in Robin's neck of the wood now. Although, don't take that as a request for you to come back to work. We're managing without you, so don't worry. We're going out to find the hunters and hopefully get some answers from them."

Baxter grimaced. He wished he was with his team. At the same time, though, he was glad he wasn't. Conversations with hunters never went well, and that was the part of the job he disliked the most.

"Let Robin know to call me, or I'll call him," Oren warned.

"I'll tell him, but I can't make promises."

"Because he's not the only one making decisions. I understand."

Baxter hesitated. He *really* didn't want to have to deal with hunters, but he also wanted answers. "I'd like to go with you to the hunters."

There was a moment of silence before Oren spoke again. "You're on vacation."

"I'm aware of that. It's not a demand, but I'd like to come. Like you guessed, this is impacting Robin and Kieran, and I want to help them."

"I doubt this will help you make a decision about whether or not you should quit the job."

"Maybe, maybe not. There's a lot I dislike about the job, but there's also a lot I like. I've been thinking, but it's hard when there's such a big problem to solve first." He'd just confirmed something was going on with the pack, but Oren already knew anyway.

"All right. You can come."

Baxter didn't know if this was the right thing to do, but hopefully, he'd get the answers Robin and Kieran needed.

"I'll text you the address. We'll see you there in an hour," Oren continued.

"I'll be there."

They hung up, and Baxter took a moment to breathe. He dreaded going back to work as much as he wanted answers, and he supposed that gave him the answer he'd needed about his future. He wanted to help and protect people, but not like this. He already had enough of the pain, blood, and horror. He'd have to find something else, but not until this was over.

He pushed away from the railing and went inside. When he'd been on the phone with Oren, he'd heard noises, so he suspected the others were back. He was right, and he found Kieran, Robin, and even Sloan talking at the table in the kitchen. They all looked up when they heard him, and Robin smiled. He looked tired, which told Baxter he was doing the right thing by going with Oren. Before he went, though, he needed to tell them what was going on.

"I was on the phone with Oren," he said. He wasn't sure how to explain what had happened without Kieran getting angry at him. "I didn't tell him what's going on with the pack, but I had asked about the drugs a few days ago. Your pack isn't the only one impacted by this. No one knows where the drugs are coming from, but they're spreading and causing people to die. It's become so bad that the council has assigned teams to several areas of the country. Oren and the team are here, and they're moving in on hunters."

"They think the hunters are behind this?" Robin asked.

"From what Oren knows, it looks like someone is targeting both vampires and shifters, possibly in the hope of starting a war that would hurt both our communities. That's why he thinks it's hunters. The team's going out to find the biggest group in the area and talk to them, and when I asked to go along, Oren agreed. I need to leave soon, but I wanted to tell you what was happening."

"It's not specific to our pack, then," Kieran said.

"It's not," Baxter confirmed. "Which means you don't have the ability to solve this by yourself. I know you wanted to do that, but this is much bigger than just you and your pack."

Kieran's shoulders slumped. "Is it bad that I'm actually relieved? I had no idea how to go about this, so I'm glad someone else is taking care of it."

"I don't think it's bad. I think it's human." Baxter gestured toward the front door. "I'm going. I hope I'll be back by morning, but don't worry if I'm not. I'll be with the team."

"I wish I could come along," Robin said. But he was the alpha mate, and he needed to stay with his pack.

"Can I come?" Sloan asked, surprising everyone.

Baxter cocked his head. "Don't you have work in the morning?"

Kieran didn't seem to have a problem with the fact that Robin was awake during the night while he had to sleep because he needed to get up in the morning. They spent a lot of time together at night. It had made Baxter wonder if he could have the same with someone, maybe with Sloan, but he hadn't dared explore the possibility. He still wasn't sure he could, and at the moment, he had other things to focus on.

"I could ask Oren," he said. "I don't think he'll have a problem with it, though." If anything, since this involved shifters, too, Sloan should be there.

Sloan got up from the armchair. "I'm coming, then."

And Baxter hoped this wouldn't be a disaster. Considering everything always went the worst way possible in his life, though, he knew not to bet on that.

Sloan was nervous as they headed out to Baxter's car. He

wanted to be involved since the pack was, but he wasn't sure this was a good idea. He'd never been with a group of vampires for long, and he hoped none of them would have a problem with it. They'd seemed nice when they'd met when Robin had moved in with Kieran, but it wasn't like they were friends.

"You're nervous," Baxter said as he drove them out of pack territory.

"Kind of. I can't help but wonder what we'll find. Why would anyone want to start a war between vampires and shifters?"

"Well, there's already a war between us. Hunters want to kill as many vampires as possible, so it would make sense for them to use shifters. They've taken a hit since their leader died."

Robin had mentioned something about that, but Sloan hadn't asked questions. Maybe he should have. "It was your team, right?"

Baxter nodded without looking away from the road. "It was. We captured the leader's son, and while he was with us, he fell in love with the medical examiner who works with our team. When Caley was taken, Darren went after him, even though he knew he'd have to face his father. He did, and he died doing so."

"I'm sorry your friend lost someone he loved."

Baxter grinned, flashing a hint of fangs in Sloan's direction. "He didn't. Most hunters are dhampirs. They hate us because they'll become vampires if they die violently, so they try to kill us to get revenge. When Darren died, he became a vampire."

There was a lot Sloan didn't know about the supernatural community. Once this was over, he'd ask Baxter all the questions he had. For now, it was better to focus on the problem at hand. "How did Darren's father die?"

"We captured him. We took him in, questioned him, and executed him."

"Wouldn't that make him a vampire?"

"It would have, but we knew what he was, and we made sure he never came back."

The words sent a chill down Sloan's spine, and he stopped asking questions. He didn't want to know what the vampires were up to.

He understood it was necessary. The lives of supernatural creatures weren't easy. There was a lot of infighting, and when they weren't fighting each other, they had to deal with humans. Often it meant violence, and it was something most shifters grew up with. It seemed vampires had to deal with the same thing, too, and it gave Sloan a sense of kinship with Baxter.

Not that he'd needed it. He already liked Baxter enough as it was.

"But hunters have never gone after other supernatural creatures as far as I know," Baxter continued. "That's why I'm not sure this is the case here. Why target both vampires and shifters? Sure, they could be trying to start a war, but how can it work when both types of creatures are dying?"

"I don't know, but it would make sense of the fact that we've been finding these bodies so close to the pack. We were lucky *we* were the ones to find them, but what if it had been someone else? What if they'd blamed the pack for those people's deaths?"

Baxter tapped his fingertips on the steering wheel. "Sure, but there was one shifter. I don't think vampires would care about shifters dying close to your pack."

That was true, too. Sloan shook his head. "We don't have any answers yet, but hopefully, we'll get them soon."

Baxter nodded. "I was surprised when you said you wanted to come along, but I have to say I'm glad. I'm a bit nervous at the thought of seeing my team again."

"Have you made your decision about whether or not you're leaving yet?"

"Not really. I don't want to go on this mission, but it's necessary to find out what's going on. I think that's what I'll struggle with if I leave. If I have a problem, I won't be able to step in in an official capacity. I'll have to call other people and let them take the lead, and I don't know if I can deal with that. On the other hand, I also won't be responsible for what's happening, and I won't have to deal with hunters and blood and all that stuff anymore."

Sloan understood, at least in part. One of the reasons he'd asked if he could go along was that he was eager to leave the responsibilities of being the pack's beta for a while. He'd be exhausted tomorrow morning, but he didn't care. He wanted some time away, and this was the best opportunity he'd had recently. Besides, it was the middle of the night. He doubted most pack members would need him now.

"Tell me about your team," he said.

Baxter arched a brow, but he didn't ask what was going through Sloan's head. "What do you want to know?"

"Well, I already know you're the new guy."

Baxter laughed. "I am, although considering I've been with them almost twenty years, I'm not actually that new. I'm the newest addition to the team, though. All of them are older than me as vampires, too."

"Did I meet all the members when they came around when Robin moved in with Kieran?"

"I think so. Let's see. There's Oren, of course. There's Ignatius, although he's been going on missions less and less recently. He fell in love, and he and his guy adopted a baby, so he's become a family man. He was there to help when Robin moved in, though."

Sloan remembered a guy who'd been showing off baby

pictures, so it had to have been him. He'd been surprised to see a vampire adopting a kid, and he had questions. "So is his child a vampire?"

"He's not. The baby is a dhampir."

"Like the hunters?"

"In part. Usually, dhampirs are human and vampire hybrids. They can be any kind of hybrid, though. In Adrian's case, his parents were a vampire and a wolf. The pack where he was found didn't want him, so Ignatius and Oscar adopted him. Oscar's a wolf, in case you're wondering."

That was surprising, although not as much as it would have been before. After all, Sloan could see how well Robin and Kieran worked together.

"Who's left?" Baxter asked, seemingly to himself. "Well, there's Renata and Gladys. Those two are always together, but I don't think they're a couple. Renata is fierce, so don't get on her bad side."

Sloan had no intention of getting on anyone's bad side.

"And the last one is Mallory. I don't think you've met Caley, but he doesn't usually work with the team. He's the medical examiner we work most often with, though."

"And he's dating Darren, an ex-hunter."

"It's a bit complicated, but yes."

It might be complicated, but it was obvious how much Baxter cared about all those people. His voice was full of affection when he told Sloan about them, and he knew they were one of the reasons Baxter was having trouble making a decision about whether or not he should leave the team. If he did, he wouldn't be able to work with them anymore. Even if he stuck around, it just wouldn't be the same.

But Sloan was curious to meet everyone again. Maybe this time they'd be able to talk more. It wasn't the right situation to be sociable, but they couldn't work all the time.

"You know, since we're talking, I was wondering why the

pack accepted Robin so easily," Baxter said.

"They didn't really have an alternative. My father, well, he was never a good alpha. I think the pack reached its limits, and when Kieran decided he wanted to take our father's place, everyone was happy. It was either accept that Robin would be the alpha mate or lose Kieran, and no one was ready for that. Besides, most of the younger members in the pack aren't as wary of vampires and other supernatural creatures as the older members are. Life has changed, and for the better. They're who we need to focus on, not the elders who have a problem with vampires."

"As long as no one hurts Robin."

"They wouldn't dare. They'd risk Kieran's wrath, and that's not something anyone wants."

"But he's not like your father. He's a good person and a good alpha. He wouldn't hurt anyone just because they insulted Robin."

"He wouldn't," Sloan confirmed. "And really, it only takes a moment talking to Robin to understand that his presence with us is a good thing. He might be a vampire, but he cares about our pack, and he's doing everything he can to keep the peace and everyone happy. I had my own doubts in the beginning, but I don't anymore. A lot of the pack doesn't care, and those who do are in the minority."

And maybe, now that Robin had opened the pack to vampires, it meant other vampires might be able to move in. Sloan glanced at Baxter, wondering what he'd do if he decided to leave his team. He wanted to help people, and plenty of people needed that here, with the pack.

Baxter found himself grinning when he reached the spot where he'd agreed to meet his team. He'd only been gone a week, but he'd missed them, which was one reason he wasn't sure he should quit his job. It would be odd not to spend most of his time with the team, but, on the other hand, he knew he wouldn't lose them. They were his family, and they'd always be there for him, just like they were there for Robin.

Baxter bounded out of the car and rushed toward Mallory. He grabbed the other vampire under the armpits and hauled him up into his arms, turning both of them around. Mallory laughed and hugged Baxter back.

"It's only been a week," he said as Baxter put him on his feet.

"It's the first time I spent a week away from you and the others since I started working with you guys. It felt like an eternity."

"Something else to consider," Oren murmured as he clasped Baxter's shoulder. "Are you sure you want to be here today?" he asked.

"I'm only leaving if you tell me to."

"We need all the help we can get." Oren's focus moved to Sloan, who'd gotten out of the car but looked uncomfortable. "I suppose he should be here, considering the pack is involved."

"They're right in the middle of it, and it's not easy."

"As long as you're sure we can trust him."

"I am." Because Robin trusted Sloan, and Baxter trusted Robin.

Besides, he and Sloan had been talking since he'd arrived, and Baxter really liked him. It wasn't just him talking with his little head, either. Sloan was hot, but he was also a nice guy, someone who'd do anything to help his brother and his pack, and a great beta. He might never have fought with a team of vampires, but he was still here, even though he was clearly uncomfortable. He wasn't going anywhere, and what he was ready to do for his pack and his brother made Baxter like him even more.

"Guys, you remember Sloan, Kieran's brother," Baxter said, gesturing at Sloan to come closer.

Sloan was still hesitant, but he approached, smiling at the team. "It's great to see all of you again."

They nodded and waved, but it was time for work, so they soon turned their attention to Oren.

They'd decided to meet a bit away from the abandoned building the hunters lived in. No one would be able to see them, and they'd have the possibility of putting their heads together before they went in. Since Baxter hadn't been with the team when they'd been briefed, he needed to gather all the information he could get.

"From what we know, there shouldn't be many hunters inside, maybe ten or twelve." Oren gestured at Mallory. "You'll enter from the front with Renata. Baxter, you're in the back with Gladys. Don't even think about ditching her. I'll know if you try. Ignatius, with me."

Baxter made an innocent face. "I'm on vacation. I'm not planning on doing anything that'll make it so that I can't continue relaxing."

Oren rolled his eyes and nodded. "Good. Sloan, I know you're here to help, but we know what we're doing. You can stick with Baxter and Gladys. Try not to get hurt, because I doubt your brother or Robin would be happy if you did."

"I'll do my best," Sloan drawled.

Baxter knew him better now, and he could tell Sloan was nervous. Whether it was because of the mission or having to trust vampires he barely knew to watch his back, Baxter didn't know. In either case, he'd make sure nothing happened to Sloan.

"We're here to get information, so try not to kill everyone. We're going to need to interrogate anyone we can find to figure out if they're behind the drugs."

Everyone looked serious now. They knew why they were

here and what they had to do.

Baxter wasn't wearing his uniform, but it didn't matter. He didn't need it to do this. He'd been going on missions with his team for two decades, and they were like a well-oiled machine, at least most of the time. Baxter just had to remember not to do anything stupid.

He wanted to impress Sloan, so he acted as seriously as he could, even though he'd always been one to joke around until the last second.

They got ready, and he, Gladys, and Sloan went around the building to the back entrance. This time, the hunters hadn't chosen a warehouse, so there were only so many places from which they could leave. Baxter supposed they could choose one of the broken windows on the ground floor, but it would take longer than using one of the doors. Besides, vampires were faster and could see better in the dark. They also only needed one hunter, possibly the one in charge. What happened to the others didn't matter.

Thankfully, Sloan didn't seem to have a problem following Baxter and Gladys's lead. He stayed back when they walked in, allowing them to take point and make sure nothing dangerous was ahead of them. When Gladys signaled she'd found a room with hunters inside, Baxter gestured at Sloan to stay where he was, and together with Gladys, they went in.

They found two hunters inside the room. They were both sitting on a beat-up couch, and to his surprise, they didn't even bother trying to escape. The bigger one placed himself in front of the other as if trying to protect her, but they stayed where they were.

"What do you want?" the hunter asked.

Baxter arched a brow, and Gladys shook her head. She had no more understanding than he did about what was going on.

"Who's your leader?" she demanded to know.

"Peter. You can find him in the next room."

Baxter was pretty sure his eyebrows had disappeared because they'd gone so far up on his forehead. Why were the hunters making this so easy? Usually, they at least put up a fight, even though they already knew they'd lose. They hated vampires because having one as a parent meant that they might become vampires, too. Baxter didn't understand their reasoning, but he supposed he didn't have to. These guys were behaving strangely, though.

"Go and see if they're lying," Gladys said. "I'll keep an eye on them."

Baxter nodded and headed out of the room. Sloan was there, looking jumpy. "What's going on?" he asked.

"I'm not sure. We found two hunters, and they told us where we could find their leader without hesitation."

Sloan blinked. "Do they usually do that?"

"Not any other hunter I've met. I don't know what's going on, but this is way too easy."

Sloan looked worried, and Baxter agreed. There was something very wrong here, and they needed to find out what it was.

He cautiously headed in the direction the hunter pointed him at. The next room didn't have a door, and when Baxter peeked in, it was to find Oren and Ignatius already there, towering over a guy flopped on a dirty mattress on the floor.

Baxter cleared his throat. Ignatius hissed and turned to face him, but he relaxed when he saw it was him.

"You're lucky I stopped," he commented.

"You'd never hurt me. What's going on?" Baxter asked.

Oren shook his head and turned back to the guy on the mattress. "This is Peter. He's the leader of this group of hunters."

It matched with what the guy in the other room had told Baxter. "I know. One of the hunters *told* me, just like he told me where to find Peter. What's going on?"

Peter snorted from his mattress. "What do you think is going on? We don't have a leader anymore. We don't even have his son. What are we supposed to do? Continue to go against vampires who easily beat and kill us? I'm not sacrificing my life for this anymore."

Baxter blinked. He'd known things were bad for the hunters after they'd lost their leader, but he'd expected someone else to step into the man's shoes. Apparently, it hadn't happened, or if it had, Peter wasn't in the loop.

"We only want answers to our questions," Oren said.

Peter shrugged. "Then ask them."

Sloan had expected more from the dangerous vampire hunters, especially after listening to some of Robin and Baxter's stories. He'd stayed in the hallway like Baxter had ordered, at least until he'd realized nothing was happening. Then, he'd peeked in, and he doubted he was in any kind of danger. The guy on the mattress didn't seem like he was willing to get to his feet, even though he was surrounded by vampires.

Sloan stepped in, and since no one told him to leave, he moved closer to the little group.

"What's going on here?" Oren asked. "Why are you so disorganized?"

"I already told you. We don't have anyone to give us orders anymore, so we make do with what we have. This has become a game of survival, and hunting vampires doesn't help with that," Peter spat out. "Many of us died, and the ones who didn't scattered around the country. With no one to lead us, we *can't* organize."

He looked angry about the situation, but not so much that he'd do something about it. Sloan supposed that was a good thing. It meant the hunters here wouldn't go after the vampires in the area.

"So since you can't fight, you decided to create drugs to kill vampires?" Oren asked.

Peter looked confused. "Drugs? I don't know what you're talking about, man. If I had drugs, I'd be taking them myself, not giving them to vampires."

Sloan couldn't know if that was the truth, but he suspected it was. Peter truly didn't seem to care what happened to vampires anymore.

"Supernatural creatures have been dying in the area. You mean to tell me your people have nothing to do with it?" Oren pushed.

Peter straightened, but he didn't try to get to his feet. "Not my group, anyway. I don't know if others have anything to do with it, but you won't find your guy here."

"Tell me about other groups in the area."

"It's just us. I'm telling you, whatever's going on with those drugs, it has nothing to do with us. There are no other hunters here."

Sloan found that hard to believe, but he'd never been informed about the situation of the vampires in town. He knew a few lived there, but vampires tended to stay away from shifters, especially wolves.

He didn't think the hunters were behind this, which meant someone else was trying to create a war between vampires and shifters. It could be any group of supernatural creatures, unfortunately. Hell, it could even be humans. Most of them weren't aware of the supernatural world, but some were, and Sloan wouldn't put it past them to try to do something with that knowledge.

Maybe now that the council was working on this, Sloan and Kieran would get answers. Sloan wanted the pack to be safe, and having someone dump bodies in front of their door wasn't helping. He was also afraid that some of the kids in the pack would eventually find this drug and try it, and that wasn't something he could allow to happen. This problem had to be solved, and as soon as possible.

"Who do you think it is, then?" Oren asked.

"How should I know? It's not like you guys haven't been trying to kill each other for hundreds of years. Just pick one group, and it's probably them."

Oren didn't look happy with that answer, but Sloan didn't disagree. Supernatural creatures *had* been trying to kill each other since they'd come into existence, and he doubted anything would change that. Things had gotten better over the past few decades, but there was still a lot of work to do.

"I should make sure all of you can never hurt anyone again," Oren said.

Peter opened his arms. "Are you going to arrest us? Because at this point, I don't think I'd mind. Do you think I like living like this?"

Oren shook his head. "We're not arresting you. You should leave this place, though. And if you do anything to any kind of supernatural creature in the area, I'll find out, and next time, I won't be so nice about it."

He turned around, not looking twice at Peter. Sloan had no intention of being left behind, so he hurried after him.

They found the rest of the team in the hallway. They didn't speak but followed Oren outside to the cars. Only there did they finally relax, and Sloan allowed himself to do the same.

"You all heard what Peter was saying?" Oren asked.

They all nodded. "You believe him?" Renata asked.

She looked ready to go back inside and kick some sense into Peter, and Sloan wouldn't be averse to watching that.

"I don't usually believe whatever hunters have to say, but in this case, I don't think he was lying. We knew they were disorganized after we got rid of Darren's father, so I'm not surprised. I just didn't expect it to be this bad. They have no will to continue fighting us."

"Isn't that a good thing?" Mallory asked.

Sloan was curious about Mallory's relationship with Baxter. Baxter had said he didn't have anyone special in his life, but the way he'd greeted Mallory, Sloan had wondered. Not that it was his place to ask or demand an explanation. He and Baxter weren't together. They were barely even friends. Sloan was interested in the vampire, but since Baxter still didn't know if he was staying or going by the end of his vacation, Sloan was afraid to take the next step. If Baxter had been anyone else, he'd already have tried to kiss him. As it was, he was scared to put his heart on the line.

It would be way too easy to lose it to Baxter.

"It's good because they won't hunt us anymore, but it still leaves us with the problem that we don't know who's behind these drugs," Oren said. "Gladys, have you heard anything from the lab?"

Gladys shook her head. "You know as much as I do at the moment."

Oren sighed. "All right. This investigation will be different. We're not going in and beating up hunters."

"Of course you guys finally have a real investigation right when I'm not working," Baxter said with a groan.

"That hasn't stopped you from coming with us today. Besides, we're going to need the pack's help."

Sloan didn't like where this was going. "I doubt any pack member will want to help you. No offense, but they're barely used to having Robin around. I don't think they'll take it well if an entire team of vampires arrives in town."

"Then you can be the one to ask them if they know anything. I know you and your brother aren't keen on letting the pack know what's going on, but at this point, I think it's necessary. It's not the hunters, which means it's going to take us a while to solve this case. They need to be careful and know what can happen to them if they take that drug. It would also be helpful to find out if any of them has seen anything at all, even things they might not have thought were strange when they happened."

He was right. He wasn't looking forward to the pack meeting they'd need to have, but they couldn't wait anymore.

It wasn't just the drugs, although that was a big part of it. It was also that someone was trying to kill as many vampires and shifters as possible or have them kill each other. The pack needed to know about it and to be careful. Sloan and Kieran had to do their jobs, no matter how little they liked it.

"It looks like we're going to be sticking around for a while," Oren added.

Sloan groaned. That was something else they'd have to tell the pack, and it was probably even worse than telling them about drugs.

CHAPTER FOUR

Baxter ignored the glaring. He was getting used to the pack members not liking his presence with them, and he didn't mind. Most pack members had been welcoming, so he could deal with the scowls, especially coming from the older members, like the lady walking past Kieran's house.

Robin had warned him about this. They hadn't dared say anything to him because he was dating Kieran, but Baxter was different, and he fully expected someone to yell at him. When and if they did, he had his answer ready — he was here on vacation and had no plans to stay.

The problem was that he'd started wondering if that was true. Well, the bit about being on vacation. He was enjoying himself for the first time since he could remember. He'd had fun with his team, too, but the worry of being sent on missions and having to deal with things he'd rather not deal with had always been there. Right now, he was worried about what was happening with the drugs, like the rest of the pack. But other than that, he'd finally relaxed, and he almost felt like the pack was home.

Some pack members weren't going to like that.

Baxter grinned and tilted his head back, looking at the sky. He was sitting on Kieran and Robin's porch in a comfortable chair, his back to the forest, but he couldn't stop himself from peeking at it every so often. He wasn't a shifter, but he'd always enjoyed nature when he was human, and he'd lost that part of himself when he'd become a vampire. Being here made him feel like he'd found it again, and he'd enjoyed several walks since he'd arrived. He'd gone on most of them alone, but Robin and even Sloan had taken some time out of their days to keep him company a few times.

But as much as Baxter wanted to stop thinking about his job, it wasn't possible. He frowned as he thought about the drugs. So far, the pack hadn't found any more bodies, but Baxter could feel the unrest in the shifters. He also knew that whoever was behind the drugs wasn't going to stop anytime soon. The pack might not have dealt with more bodies, but the number of people who died because of the drugs around the country had gone up. Oren kept Baxter updated, and he was starting to worry, too. Baxter wanted to solve this mystery, and maybe, once he was able to quit his job, settle down.

He looked at the house again. He could hear Sloan and Kieran talking inside, and he wanted to join them. More than that, he wanted to see Sloan. He hadn't yet today, and he was excited, which could only mean one thing.

He had a crush on Sloan.

Baxter wasn't surprised. He'd liked Sloan since the first time they'd met. Back then, he hadn't said anything, and he still hadn't. He didn't know what he was doing with his life yet, but he was tempted to stick around. He didn't have to live with the pack, but he could settle down in town. Of course, he'd have to find out if Sloan liked him, too. Baxter wasn't leaving his job because of a guy, but it would be good to have someone in his life once he did.

The back door opened, causing Baxter to look at it again. He smiled when Sloan stepped out of the house.

"I see you're taking your vacation time very seriously," Sloan teased.

He looked tired, just like Kieran and even Robin these days. Baxter suspected they were reaching the end of their patience with this case, and he didn't blame them. He had enough worries with just the case, and he didn't have to think about the pack and the wolves. It couldn't be easy for any of them, and he admired how resilient and strong they were.

He got up from his chair and smiled gently. "I am. I haven't taken a vacation in twenty years, so I'm making the most of it. You look like you need one, too."

Sloan chuckled darkly. "I wish I could go on vacation."

But he couldn't because of the drugs and because he needed to keep the pack safe.

"Well, you might not be able to take a vacation, but you could take the rest of the evening off. What were you going to do now?"

"Go home and go over what we have on the case."

"It's already nine PM. Why don't you take the rest of the evening off, relax for a few hours, and go to bed early?" Kieran and Sloan had spent a lot of time with Robin and Baxter, which meant their schedules were all over the place.

Sloan grimaced. "It's tempting, but I really shouldn't. This is getting complicated."

"I agree, but a few hours away from this case should be fine. Besides, you won't be able to do anything if you're exhausted, and you obviously are."

"You know how to seduce a man."

Baxter grinned. "Trust me. When I seduce you, you'll know I am." It was a risk to say that to Sloan's face, but maybe it was time to get serious about this.

Sloan looked taken aback, but not in a bad way. He blinked, and his lips stretched into a smile. "Is that something you're planning on doing, then?" he asked.

"Maybe. For a start, why don't I walk you home?"

"You don't have to. Nothing's going to happen to me in the few feet from my brother's house to mine."

"I never said anything about something happening to you. I just want to walk you home."

"Then, by all means."

Sloan gestured at the porch steps, and Baxter hopped down. Sloan followed him more slowly, and together, they started walking.

Baxter had explored pack territory in the first few days after he'd arrived. It had been almost two weeks now, and he knew the place well. He'd wanted to be sure he knew every pack member in case someone who shouldn't be here snuck in, and to know the layout of the place, just in case something happened. He knew where Sloan's house was, even though he'd never been inside.

"Will you be going back to work soon, then?" Sloan asked.

"I don't think so. I haven't resigned from my position yet because I want to solve this drug thing first. My vacation time is going to end soon, but Oren already agreed that I need to stay here."

"Not that I'm not happy to have you here a bit longer, but is that really necessary? Shouldn't you be going back to your team?"

"I would if my leader wanted me to, but I already told Oren I wouldn't stick around once this was over. I think he suspected that would be the case, and he wasn't surprised, but he knows I want to see the end of this first. I want the pack to be safe."

Sloan nodded. "I can see that. I have to say I'm surprised."

"Why, because I'm a vampire?"

"Not really. Robin's a vampire, too, and he cares about the pack. No, it's because we're nothing to you."

Baxter glanced at Sloan. "That's not true," he murmured.

They reached Sloan's house, which was only a few feet away from Kieran's. Maybe now was the time to tell Sloan how much he liked him. Baxter didn't know if anything would happen between them, especially considering the circumstances, but it wouldn't be a bad thing for Sloan to be aware of his feelings. Maybe he'd give Baxter one more reason to stick around.

"What the fuck are you doing with that vampire?" a harsh voice asked.

Baxter's first instinct was to place himself in front of Sloan. He faced the man striding toward them, recognizing him even though he'd never talked to him. Kieran and Sloan both looked like him, although Baxter doubted they'd age as badly as he had.

The man had bloodshot eyes as if he hadn't been sleeping. His clothes were dirty and smelled, even though he wasn't anywhere close to Baxter. They didn't sit well on his body, as if he'd had them a while and had lost weight, but his face was swollen. His graying hair was all over the place, and he made it worse when he raked his hands through it.

"What do you want?" Sloan asked, sounding resigned.

His father stopped in front of Baxter. He tried to walk around him, but Baxter followed him, making clear he wouldn't allow him to touch Sloan. If he wanted to try anything, he'd have to go through Baxter, and Baxter was confident he'd be the one to win. He didn't want to fight with Sloan's father, but if he had to, he would. He was a protector, and he *would* protect Sloan.

Sloan had no will or energy to deal with his father, but he knew his dad wasn't going anywhere before saying what he wanted to stay. "Just speak," he said with a sigh.

He was surprised at the way Baxter stood between him and his father, although maybe he shouldn't be. He and Baxter had talked enough that he knew the guy now, so he was aware of the fact that Baxter wanted to protect people. It was ingrained in him, and it always would be, even when he stopped being an enforcer.

"I want to talk to you alone, without this guy." The last

word dripped contempt and hatred.

It made Sloan wince, but Baxter didn't even react. It was almost as if he was used to it, and Sloan suspected that in some situations, he was. It was a pity. He never wanted Baxter to feel hated or rejected.

Sloan put a hand on the small of Baxter's back and walked to stand next to him. His father's eyes narrowed when he noticed the touch, but before he could say anything, Sloan stopped him.

"Yes, I know. Vampires are evil, and they're going to get all of us killed. You've been telling me that every chance you've had since Robin arrived. But you're not the alpha anymore. You're not the one who makes decisions, and Baxter is allowed to stay. He's also a good guy, and he's helping the pack. You really should let go of the hatred and look at the future rather than the past. Vampires never hurt you or the pack, so why don't you try seeing them as the people they are instead of the monsters you've always imagined in your head?"

"This won't end well," his father said, wagging a finger at Sloan's face. "They're going to kill all of us, and it'll be yours and your brother's fault. I won't allow them to hurt my pack. Mark my words."

With that, he turned around and stomped away. Sloan waited for a moment, watching him go. He'd accepted the fact that his father would never be in his life again, and he didn't care. He understood that some people were wary of vampires and might have a good reason to be, but that didn't mean they shouldn't see every vampire as an individual. He didn't want vampires to hate all werewolves and shifters. He'd never done anything to any of them, and he didn't hate all vampires, or any vampire at all, really.

"I'm sorry," Baxter whispered.

Sloan started taking his hand away, but he liked touching

Baxter. He liked being close to the vampire, and he'd been thinking about it for a while now, since the first time he and Baxter had met. He didn't know if Baxter would stay with the pack after he resigned, but maybe Sloan could show him that he'd have a good reason to if he wanted to.

He turned to face Baxter and used his hold on him to pull him into his arms. Baxter blinked, but the corner of his lips curled into a smile. When Sloan kissed him, Baxter didn't resist or try to pull away. Instead, he leaned closer, pressing his hands against Sloan's chest.

Their lips met. The kiss was gentle and exploring, but it held the promise of heat and so much more. Sloan didn't go for that just then. It was enough for him to kiss Baxter here in the forest, under the stars.

Baxter's lips were soft. They moved generously, and when Sloan poked at them with his tongue, they opened and welcomed him inside. He licked his way into Baxter's mouth, smiling at the sound that left Baxter's body.

"It sounds like you're enjoying this," he said.

"I am, very much so," Baxter said. "I was wondering if it would happen."

"I didn't know you wanted it until now."

Baxter chuckled and pressed their foreheads together. "I thought I'd been obvious, but I've never been great at flirting. I did tell you I wanted to seduce you, though."

"You did. I suppose I needed to give you the opportunity to do it."

"And instead, it looks like you were the one to seduce me."

Sloan hesitated. He didn't want Baxter to think he was only in this for the sex, but he'd been dying to get his hands on the guy, and he couldn't wait anymore. Besides, there was much more than sex in this, but it didn't mean sex couldn't be part of it.

"Do you want to come in?" he whispered.

Baxter didn't even hesitate. "I'd love to."

Sloan took his hand and pulled him toward the house. He looked around, wondering if his father had seen them, but he was nowhere to be seen. That didn't mean he hadn't been spying, but Sloan didn't care.

He didn't care about anyone seeing him and Baxter together. He wasn't ashamed of liking a vampire, and he wouldn't hesitate to tell people how much he cared for Baxter. He and Baxter needed to have a conversation about it, but that could wait until tomorrow.

They stumbled inside the house, and Sloan hesitated. "Bedroom?" he asked.

Baxter nodded eagerly. "Please. Or the couch. We could do it on the floor, but it wouldn't be comfortable."

Sloan laughed and pulled Baxter along. He couldn't remember the last time he'd laughed so much, and not just in this situation. He'd been smiling a lot more since Baxter had arrived, even with the dead bodies and drugs. Baxter lit up Sloan's life, and Sloan wanted more of that.

He hadn't made his bed this morning, and there were dirty clothes on the floor, but he didn't care. He doubted Baxter would, either. They both made a beeline for the bed, still holding hands, and flopped onto it. Sloan pulled Baxter to him, and Baxter rolled right into his arms and kissed him again.

Sloan felt like a teenager as he fumbled with Baxter's jeans. He managed to get them open and pushed his hand inside, grinning when Baxter moaned loudly.

Sloan wrapped his fingers around Baxter's cock and pulled. Baxter was already hard, and he was hot, his skin silky against Sloan's rough hands. He didn't seem to care about that, and he pushed into Sloan's hold.

"I can't let you have all the fun," Baxter murmured.

He undid Sloan's pants with more grace than Sloan had, then pushed them down Sloan's hips. Sloan wanted more, but he wasn't sure Baxter would be comfortable with getting entirely naked during their first time together. Sloan was a shifter, so he didn't have a problem being naked with people, but Baxter was a vampire.

Still, Sloan wanted Baxter naked, and he supposed he might as well ask. He pressed kisses on Baxter's neck up to his ear, then, once he was there, he whispered, "Want you naked."

Baxter nodded so enthusiastically that he almost head-butted Sloan in the nose. Sloan jerked back at the last moment and laughed, but the sound died on his lips when Baxter started pulling his t-shirt off.

Sloan had been sneaking peeks at Baxter's body every time he could since Baxter had arrived, but now, as Baxter's skin was revealed, he knew how much he'd missed by only seeing him with his clothes on. Baxter's limbs were long and his skin pale, except where it was dotted with freckles — and there were a lot of them.

They peppered Baxter's shoulders and the top of his chest, down his arms, and his stomach. There were fewer of them there and on his legs, but Sloan still wanted to kiss and lick every single one of them. It was an impossible task, but if he had anything to say about it, he'd have years to complete it.

He slid down Baxter's body as Baxter pushed his jeans down his legs. Sloan helped with that, throwing them off the bed and staring at the long cock in front of him. It was flushed red and looked so good that Sloan couldn't resist and licked the head.

Baxter shuddered. "Not like this," he whispered, reaching for Sloan.

Sloan was more than happy to let him move him like he wanted. He wasn't surprised when he ended up naked, too. Then Baxter pushed him until he was on his side, and he stretched out beside him, his head toward Sloan's feet.

Sloan could work with that.

He wrapped his fingers around Baxter's cock and took it into his mouth. He'd never been crazy about this position, mostly because it was hard to focus on doing anything when someone was sucking him off. Baxter, especially, was driving him nuts, but Sloan wanted him to enjoy this as much as he was, so he did his best. He sucked and licked, and while sometimes he had to stop because of what Baxter was doing to him, he made sure it wasn't for long.

He also made sure to touch every inch of Baxter's body he could reach, going as far as slipping his finger in the crack of Baxter's ass cheeks. Baxter didn't seem to mind. If anything, he seemed to enjoy it since he started thrusting into Sloan's mouth and pushing back against his finger with the next movement.

Sloan let go of Baxter's cock, quickly sucked on his fingers, then went right back to it. At the same time, he pushed a finger into Baxter's ass.

Baxter cried out, then swallowed Sloan's cock. He didn't seem to have a gag reflex, and Sloan was reaching the end of what he could stand without coming. He didn't want to come alone, though, so he found Baxter's prostate. It took him a few tries, but once he did, Baxter went off like a rocket. He jerked and came down Sloan's throat, thrusting his hips forward so much that Sloan sputtered. He didn't push Baxter away, though. He didn't want to.

After all of this, it only took Sloan a few seconds to come, too. Baxter's cock was still in his mouth, and he could feel it twitch at the same time as Baxter's ass tightened around his finger.

Sloan wanted to stay here forever, but it wasn't possible. Both he and Baxter flopped away from each other, trying to get their breath back. Sloan wondered if Baxter was going to leave now that they were done. He was relieved when instead of doing that, Baxter rolled toward him and cuddled against his side. Sloan wrapped an arm around Baxter's shoulders and held him close, praying this wouldn't be the only chance they'd have to do this.

Baxter was relieved Sloan wasn't kicking him out of bed. He hadn't been sure, because not everyone was a cuddler, but it seemed he wasn't going anywhere just yet.

"This was a long time coming," Sloan murmured.

"We should have done it sooner," Baxter agreed.

Sloan sighed. "We would have without this mess with the drugs. I don't know what to do or how to help my brother and the pack, and it's driving me nuts."

Baxter had been thinking about this, and he had an idea, but he doubted Sloan would like it. He'd have to talk to the others first—or maybe not. Because Baxter knew Oren wouldn't be happy with this, either. He'd told Baxter not to do anything stupid, but sometimes, it was the only way to get results.

He propped himself up on his elbow and looked down at Sloan. "I have an idea, but I need you to listen to me before saying anything."

"I'm not going to like whatever you have to say, am I?"

"Probably not. I'm new in town. Your pack knows me, but I haven't been into town yet, except for a few quick visits. I want to go there and look for the drugs."

Sloan sat up, but he didn't push Baxter away, which was a relief. "You mean you want to act like a buyer?"

"If the people selling the drugs don't associate me with your pack, they might sell me the drugs. Once I know who they are, we can deal with it."

"No."

Baxter had expected that. "I'm not one of your pack

members," he said gently. "You can't stop me from doing this, and you can't order me around."

"I can't, but Oren could. I'll call him if you go."

And him, Baxter would have to obey. Baxter needed to convince Sloan this was the only way to do this.

He sat up and crossed his legs, then pulled the sheet over his groin. "You were just saying that you don't know what to do. I do. I can do this. I'm a trained enforcer, and I've been doing this kind of thing for the past twenty years. Think about it, please. It would be the perfect way to finally find out who's behind the drugs and get rid of them. Isn't that what you want?"

"It is, but I don't want you to get hurt, either. There's only one way this will end, and it's not well."

"But if I find out who's selling the drugs, we can arrest them and get answers. I don't think there's another way out of this. We *have* to stop what's happening, and so far, you haven't had a better idea. No one has."

Sloan rubbed his face with both his hands. "So you expect me to put you into danger. Look, I understand you're an enforcer, but we're shifters. You're not part of the pack, which means you don't owe us anything."

Baxter glared and crossed his arms over his chest. "So you think I should just leave and ignore what's going on? I might not be a pack member, but that doesn't mean I don't care about you, Robin, or Kieran. If I can do anything to help you, I will, and this is the best and *only* way to make that happen."

Sloan glared right back, but Baxter thought he was softening. He had to see this was the only way to find out what was going on. They could wait for the council and the team to find more information, but they'd been poking around for a week now, and they still had no more answers than they did in the beginning. The hunters didn't seem to be at fault, but then who was?

It was probably a group of people. It would be too much work for only one or two people to create the drugs and distribute them. Since they were working together and against other supernatural creatures, they had to belong to this world. It could be humans, but Baxter doubted they'd go about it this way.

It would be dangerous to go against them, but they didn't have a choice.

"If you're going, I'm coming with you."

Baxter shook his head. "You can't. Someone is bound to recognize you, especially if they've been hanging around town. They'd know something is going on, because there's no way the alpha's beta, who's also his brother, would go around buying drugs, especially with the three bodies you've already found. I'm telling you, whoever is doing this is part of a bigger supernatural group. They killed people, then placed their bodies either as a warning to the pack or as a way to frame you."

"All of this means they're dangerous, and I won't let you do this on your own."

"Is it because of what we just did?" Baxter didn't expect a declaration of eternal love, but he wanted to know where he stood with Sloan, especially if he was going to go get those drugs. It would be dangerous, and it would be good to have something to come back to.

To have *someone* to come back to.

Baxter never had. In the beginning, he'd had to deal with being turned and becoming an enforcer. It had taken all his time and energy, and he hadn't had much time for a relationship. He'd tried a few times, but it hadn't worked out. He felt ready for one now, especially since he was planning on quitting his job, and he didn't want to ruin what he and Sloan had.

"In part, but mostly it's because I care about you. I don't know what we're doing, but I want to see where it goes, and

I won't be able to if you get yourself killed. I can hide in the car or stay away, but I'm not letting you go on your own," Sloan insisted. "It's too dangerous. I want to be there so I can step in if something happens and you need help. And yes, I know you're a trained enforcer and that you've done this hundreds of times, but it doesn't change my decision. I'm not your beta, but I can call Oren, and we both know you don't want that to happen."

Even though it would be the smartest thing to do.

Oren wouldn't be happy with the plan, even though he'd have to admit it was the only way they could go about this. But Baxter had no intention of calling Oren. He got out of bed, looking for his clothes.

"What are you doing?" Sloan asked.

"Getting dressed. Aren't we heading out?"

"You mean you want to do this now?"

"Why wait? Since some of the victims were vampires, it means the dealer probably sells at night, too. If I had to guess, he's probably at clubs and places where vampires can find people willing to let them drink their blood."

"Do you drink from people?" Sloan asked.

At least he wasn't telling Baxter to stop. "Sometimes. Some vampires treat it as if they're drinking from a juice box, but feeding is more intimate to me. I don't like to do it with people I don't know, so I don't do it often. That's what bottled blood is for."

"When do you do it, then?"

"Usually, when I'm dating someone, and it's serious." Which meant that Baxter hadn't fed on anyone for a while. It had only happened once or twice, and every time, he'd thought the relationship was more serious than it actually was.

"Do you drink from werewolves? Shifters?"

Baxter finished pulling his t-shirt down and smiled at

Sloan. "I would if I was dating one and he was amenable to it."

Sloan nodded. He was still sitting in bed, but he shook himself and grabbed his clothes. "All right. Since you insist on doing this tonight, we might as well head out."

"You don't have to come with me." Baxter tried again, but he already knew it wouldn't work.

"If you're not going to call your team or even Robin and Kieran, I'm coming."

Baxter was relieved he wouldn't be on his own, but he was also afraid something would happen to Sloan.

Baxter couldn't promise everything would be okay or that he'd stay out of trouble. He'd never been one to do that, and he wasn't going to start now.

Sloan liked this idea less and less as they drove toward town. The problem was that it made sense. They'd been trying to find who was behind these drugs, but Baxter seemed to be the only one who'd nailed the characteristics of those people.

It had to be a large group, which meant they were powerful. They also had money, since they were making drugs but losing the people who bought them every time someone died. Sloan doubted they expected to make any kind of money out of this since their goal was to kill supernatural creatures. All of it meant that whoever it was, they were probably too powerful for the pack to take on.

They'd need the council. Sloan wasn't happy about that, but he thought he could deal with it, especially after what had just happened with Baxter. He'd been meeting more vampires than he ever expected to meet in his life, but they were all good people. They were fighters, and they'd fight with the pack if they had to.

He hoped they wouldn't.

"Where are we going, then?" Baxter asked.

Sloan was driving, since he was from around here and knew where supernatural creatures gathered at night. "There's a club right at the edge of town. I've never been because it's not my kind of scene, but I've been told vampires go there. There are antiviolence spells over it, so the different creatures can't hurt each other, but I suppose that selling drugs to someone doesn't count as hurting them."

"They do the hurting themselves when they take them," Baxter said softly.

And Sloan was afraid something like this was going to happen to Baxter. What if the people who tried selling him the drugs forced him to take them in front of them? As far as Sloan knew, there was no coming back once you took the pills, and he didn't want anything to happen to Baxter.

"I'll be fine," Baxter promised.

Sloan wished he could believe him.

They stayed silent as they reached the club. Sloan wasn't about to wait outside, and with so many people inside, he doubted anyone would notice him. He'd stay in the shadows and watch Baxter, even though it would cost him to do so.

"Let me know if you need any kind of help," he told Baxter before they left the car.

"I promise. Keep your eyes open, and let me know if you see anything strange."

"We shouldn't be doing this on our own."

Baxter grinned and quickly kissed Sloan's cheek. "Probably not, but it's too late to change it now."

He headed toward the club, and Sloan scrambled to go after him. He slipped into the club just behind Baxter, and while Baxter made a beeline for the dance floor, Sloan chose a spot against the wall. It was just behind a pillar, so he was relatively hidden, but he could still keep an eye on Baxter.

And keep an eye on him, he did.

There was no looking away, especially once Baxter started dancing. All of the clumsiness that endeared him so much to Sloan was gone as he seamlessly moved his hips to the rhythm of the music. Sloan's mouth was dry, and he had to remind himself why they were here. He shouldn't be drooling all over Baxter. Instead, he needed to keep an eye out for anyone who might create trouble.

Sloan was terrified, but Baxter didn't seem to have that problem. He looked perfectly at ease on the dance floor, even when guys and girls came closer to dance with him. He did so with a few, mostly with women. They hadn't talked about their sexualities, so Baxter might be bisexual, but maybe he just thought they'd be less dangerous. Or maybe Sloan was reading too much into this. He had no idea.

Instead of staring at Baxter the entire time—even though he wanted to—Sloan looked around. His gaze caught on a small group of people, most of them guys. They were looking around as if searching for something, which was what caught Sloan's interest. One of them exchanged words, then money, with one of the dancers. The girl who'd bought whatever the guys were selling disappeared down a hallway, maybe to the bathroom.

Sloan was tempted to go after them and get the drugs she might have bought from her, but he stayed where he was. He couldn't save the entire world, but he *could* save Baxter if Baxter needed him to.

The group of guys disbanded and lost themselves in the crowd. Several ended up on the dance floor, and when one moved closer to Baxter, Sloan pushed away from the wall and headed in that direction. He made sure not to get too close, but he wanted to know what was going on.

The guy grabbed Baxter's hips and pulled him close in a hard gesture. Instead of pushing him away, Baxter laughed and leaned closer. He seemed interested in whatever the guy was saying, and even though Sloan knew it was all for show, he was still pissed. He knew Baxter didn't want this guy to touch him, and it wasn't right that he had to go along with it because of this case. Sloan wished he could step in and tell the guy to fuck off, but he didn't want to have to do this a second time, and he didn't think Baxter did, either.

He didn't think he'd be able to watch Baxter put himself through this a second time.

When Baxter and the guy headed toward the exit, Sloan trailed behind them. He tried to appear as if he was just going to his car, but he wasn't sure he was doing a good job. He didn't care. The only thing he cared about was Baxter.

Baxter and the guy got outside before Sloan, and when Sloan followed them, it took him a moment to see them. He almost panicked, but then he realized that Baxter had put them in sight of the cameras close to the door. Sloan didn't know if the drug dealer had noticed, but he didn't seem to care as he leaned closer to Baxter and took something from his jeans pocket. He held it out, and Baxter took it with two fingers, looking both curious and nervous. Sloan couldn't help but be impressed. Baxter was a great actor.

"What's it going to do to me?" Baxter asked.

Sloan moved even closer, trying not to make any kind of noise. The drug dealer had his back to him, thankfully, but if he was a supernatural creature, he might still notice Sloan was there.

"It'll make you fly, baby. Don't you want to fly?" the drug dealer asked.

Baxter licked his lips. "And you're sure it's not danger-ous?"

"I promise it's not. This was created for vampires. See the fangs? That means you can trust it."

Sloan almost scoffed. This guy really wanted Baxter dead if he was pushing so hard.

"You've been selling a lot of these?"

"Yeah. That means that if you want it, you need to take it now. What do you say? We could go back to my apartment after you take it and have fun."

Sloan had enough. He quickly moved closer, grabbed the dealer's arm, and pulled him away from Baxter and toward him. At the same time, Baxter moved forward. He hooked his arm around the dealer's throat from behind and squeezed. The guy froze.

"I work for the vampire council," Baxter said in a low voice that sent a thrill down Sloan's back. "You've been selling drugs to vampires and shifters, drugs that killed them. You're going to tell me who your boss is, and you're going to do it now."

Sloan would have done anything Baxter wanted if he'd asked it in that tone, but obviously, the drug dealer didn't feel the same way. He laughed, then, as Sloan watched him, he started shifting.

It wouldn't have been a problem if his shifted form hadn't been so big. Baxter had to let go, as did Sloan. He snatched Baxter and pulled him closer, and together they stared at the giant lizard that appeared in front of them.

"Fuck," Baxter rasped out. "He's a dragon shifter."

He could have eaten them in one movement, but thankfully, he didn't seem to want to do that. Instead, he opened his wings, pushed himself into the air, and flew away.

The only thing Baxter and Sloan could do was stare until he disappeared from sight.

CHAPTER FIVE

"A freaking dragon. Can you believe it?" Baxter asked. He was bouncing in the passenger seat of Sloan's car. He couldn't help himself. They'd found one of the dealers, and he was a freaking *dragon* shifter.

"I wasn't even sure they still existed," Sloan said.

He didn't sound as excited as Baxter, making Baxter feel guilty. Of course Sloan wasn't excited. The dragons had targeted his pack, and they still didn't know why. Besides, dragons would be tricky to deal with. They were huge when they shifted, lived in clans, and were hoarders when it came to money, so they were usually rich and basically immortal. They lived a long time, like vampires, and usually they stayed out of the business of other packs and shifter groups. Why these dragons had decided to start dealing drugs deadly to vampires and shifters was a mystery, and Baxter suspected they wouldn't like what they'd discovered.

"Aren't you used to seeing weird things?" Sloan asked with a smile.

Baxter grinned at him. They could start thinking about the consequences of what they'd found out later. "I am. I mean, in my twenty years, I've fought against pretty much every supernatural creature you can think of."

"Really? Can you tell me which ones?"

"Well, werewolves and vampires, of course. Griffins. Harpies, fae people, witches, selkies." Baxter counted on his fingers as he spoke. "Oh, and that one time, a satyr. It's hard to remember all of them."

"Because you've been an enforcer for twenty years."

"Yeah. And most of the time, we deal with vampires. But I'd never seen a dragon shifter until tonight, and I can only imagine how complicated it's going to be to deal with an entire clan of them. I'm not looking forward to telling Oren about this."

"That wouldn't be because you did something he wouldn't have wanted you to do?"

"Not just that. I mean he's not going to be happy when I tell him what I did, but I'm not going to hide it, not when I know who's behind all of this."

Sloan sighed. "I wonder why they're doing this. I mean, it's not like the pack has done anything to them. We didn't even know they existed."

"I don't think there's a way for us to find out without talking to them, and I doubt they'll want to do that. I suppose we'll see."

But Baxter was worried. He didn't know if they'd be able to do anything about the dragon shifters. They were going to try, but it didn't mean they'd win.

They continued chatting about everything but the dragon shifters as Sloan drove them back to the pack. It didn't take long, and instead of going to his house, he parked in front of Kieran's place. Baxter took his phone out of his pocket as they reached the front door. He let Sloan knock on the door and guide him in as he called Oren.

"Baxter?" Oren said when he answered.

"Hold on. Sloan and I are about to talk to Kieran and Robin about something that happened tonight. I wanted you to be able to hear it, too."

Robin's eyes narrowed. "What have you done?" he asked Baxter.

Baxter shook his head. "Nothing."

Sloan snorted. "It wasn't nothing," he said. "But I was with him, if it makes you feel better."

"I'm not sure it does. Come on, sit down. Baxter, do you want some blood?"

"Not yet. I'll get some before going to bed later."

It wouldn't be long before he and Robin went to sleep. He supposed Kieran and Sloan would follow their lead, at least for tonight. The sun was still hidden beyond the trees, but Baxter was exhausted. This needed to be done first. He briefly wondered if maybe Sloan would want him to go home with him, but he wasn't about to ask, not now, not here.

Robin had disappeared down the hallway to wake up Kieran, but thankfully, it didn't take long for the alpha to join them. He was wearing pajama pants and a t-shirt, and his cheek was creased with the imprint of his pillow. His eyes were blurry, but he looked strong and steady, and Baxter trusted him.

Robin made a beeline for the coffee pot, and Baxter wondered if they should wait until Kieran and Sloan had coffee in front of them, but Kieran would have none of it. "Talk," he ordered.

Baxter put his phone on speaker and placed it in front of himself on the table. "Oren is on the line," he explained.

Kieran nodded and gestured at him to continue speaking, so he did.

Baxter cleared his throat. "Sloan and I went out tonight. He took me to the club frequented by vampires."

"Midnight," Sloan interrupted.

Baxter hadn't even noticed that was the club's name, but whoever the owner was, he wasn't very inventive. "There were a lot of supernatural creatures there, including vampires, but they're not the people selling drugs. One of the dealers approached me. He tried to get me to take some of those pills with the fangs printed on them."

"Please tell me you didn't," Robin begged.

"I don't want to die, so no. Sloan and I confronted the guy, or at least, we tried to. I thought we could maybe drag him here and get answers out of him, but he shifted and flew away."

"What kind of shifter flies?" Kieran asked.

"No shifter you want to deal with," Oren's voice came from the phone. "You recognized the species, Baxter?"

"It would have been impossible not to. We're dealing with dragon shifters."

There was a moment of silence as everyone digested that. Even with all the creatures Baxter had dealt with, he'd never met a dragon shifter, so there was nothing he could add.

"I've met dragons in the past," Robin said.

"So have I," Oren added. "They're not easy to deal with. This isn't good."

"Can you tell me why?" Kieran asked.

Robin placed two mugs of coffee on the table and a stainless steel bottle in front of Baxter before slipping into the chair next to Kieran's. "They hate pretty much everyone. It's not like vampires and werewolves, who hate each other. Dragons hate all supernatural creatures, along with humans. They think they're superior, and in a way, they are. They want to rule, and the only reason they haven't is that there are so few of them. They don't reproduce easily, even though they're immortal, or maybe because of it."

Baxter opened the bottle and took a sip. Robin had warmed the blood, and Baxter sighed in pleasure as he finally allowed himself to relax.

"I suppose not all of them are like that," Kieran commented.

"Probably not, but there are very few of them around. They live in clans, and they're hoarders. Generally, it's money, although not always. Not that I've ever seen a dragon's hoard. I'm sure you can imagine how territorial they are about that.

They don't even allow other dragons to see it, usually."

"Can we be sure this dragon clan is the one spreading these drugs?" Oren asked.

"I suppose we can't," Baxter intervened. "I mean, the guy who tried to drug me was a dragon shifter, but I don't know about the others he was talking with in the club. I also don't know where he lives and if his clan is behind all of this. The only thing I can tell you is that the guy who tried to give me those drugs tonight was a dragon shifter. He shifted and flew away."

"Did you find anything in the clothes he left behind?"

Once Baxter had recovered from his shock at seeing a dragon, he'd picked up the clothes and had carried them to the car, just in case. "A phone, ID, and several plastic bags containing the drugs. There was quite a bit of money in the wallet."

"Snap pictures of everything and send them to me. The team and I will come over tomorrow night."

Baxter was relieved he and the pack wouldn't have to face these dragons on their own. Still, he wasn't sure his team would be enough, not against a bunch of dragons.

"Is there anything I can do right now?" Kieran asked.

"I doubt it," Oren told him. "I know you want to protect your pack, but it's better to stay away from these dragons. They're dangerous. I wouldn't try to contact them if I were you."

"I don't know if I can stay back and let them continue doing this."

"Warn your pack that they're in the area. Hopefully, we'll have more answers by tomorrow, and we'll be able to start planning what the next step will be. In the meantime, go on with your life."

Baxter knew from experience that it was easier said than done, but they didn't have a choice.

Sloan still had a hard time believing what he'd seen, but he couldn't deny it. At the moment, though, he was more worried about the pack and how they'd take the news than about the dragons.

They'd wanted answers, and now Sloan and Kieran could give them some. The problem was that they wouldn't be the answers the pack wanted. Everyone here wanted to hear that they were safe and that they could go on with their lives, but that wasn't the case. Sloan didn't want to live in fear, but he couldn't deny something was going on and that the pack needed to be careful.

Everyone was scared, and Sloan had no doubt that was why in the past few days he'd started hearing some people wondering if Kieran was a good choice as their alpha. No one could deny that Sloan and Kieran's father would have done an even worse job of this, but still. Kieran was doing everything he could without results. It was normal for the pack to be worried, but Sloan disliked the talk about finding someone better. There was no one better than Kieran and Robin to lead the pack, and no one who would know what to do in this situation.

But maybe Kieran should choose someone else as his beta. He could find someone with more experience, something Sloan sorely lacked. He'd been doing his best, too, but it didn't feel like enough, especially in light of what he and Baxter had found tonight.

Kieran clasped Sloan's shoulder. "You should go home," he murmured.

Robin and Baxter were still talking with Oren, but Sloan had stopped listening. They weren't saying anything he didn't already know and that hadn't been said several times already tonight.

Sloan stretched. He was exhausted, and there would be no going to work for him tomorrow morning. Hell, it was *already* tomorrow morning. The only thing he wanted to do was drag Baxter into bed and stay there for a week, possibly longer.

"I feel like we should do something," he told his brother.

"I understand that, but I don't think there's anything we *can* do at the moment. Oren is right. The pack isn't equipped to deal with dragons, and I can't imagine where to start anyway. Both of us need sleep, as do Baxter and Robin. Besides, the dragons aren't our only problem. We need to deal with the pack, and they won't wait until we're rested to come knock on our doors."

Sloan would bite anyone who came knocking today, but he couldn't exactly say that out loud. Now more than ever, he regretted accepting the beta job, and while he knew Kieran would let him step down if he asked, he didn't. He and his brother were in this together, no matter how much they disliked it.

"But I'm curious to know," Kieran continued. "What were you and Baxter doing in town at this hour of the night? Were you showing him around? Because I know that club isn't your scene."

Sloan grimaced. Kieran wasn't going to like this, but he wasn't going to lie. "Baxter wanted to go on his own, kind of undercover. He said that since no one in town knew him, it would be easy to get someone to sell him the drugs. He wanted to grab the dealer and interrogate him. And he was right. That guy didn't hesitate to offer him those drugs, and he was pushy about it. If Baxter hadn't known what was going on, he might have tried, just to get that guy off his back. It's not like many drugs can kill vampires."

"You should have told me."

"I should have, but Baxter was going out there, whether or not I went with him. I couldn't allow him to do it on his own."

Kieran cocked his head. He was staring at Sloan, and Sloan knew he was reading him. He didn't mind his brother knowing that he and Baxter were together, but the problem was that Sloan wasn't sure they were. He liked Baxter and wanted to be with him, but would Baxter stick around once this was over? Even if he quit his job, that didn't mean he'd stay in town. He didn't have a reason to. As a vampire, he could travel all over the world. He could explore what life had to offer him, and staying in town sounded kind of boring when Sloan thought about it. Baxter was immortal, and surely his life would be better lived out there.

"You and Baxter were together tonight," Kieran said.

Which reminded Sloan of another problem. "We were," he confirmed. "And Dad confronted me. Baxter was there."

Kieran groaned and rubbed his face. "That's the last thing I need. What did he want?"

"The usual. He hates vampires. They're going to eat all of us, that kind of thing. I told him to fuck off, but you know how he is. He's not going to stop." And it could become a problem. Sloan had no doubt it would, eventually, but he prayed they'd deal with the dragons first. He didn't have the energy to deal with two big problems at the moment.

"I should probably talk to him," Kieran murmured.

"I don't know if it would help. He doesn't want the vampires to be here, and he wants everyone to know that."

"There's no way for anyone not to be aware of it. He's been pretty vocal about it. We just can't afford for him to create more trouble, not with dragons targeting us. We're going to have to do something about him before this gets out of hand." Kieran got to his feet. "But not tonight. Come on. The three of you need to go to bed."

"It *is* late," Oren said on the phone. "Baxter, Robin, I'll talk to you tomorrow. Get some rest. You're going to need it."

Everyone said their goodbyes. Sloan stayed where he was

for a moment, rubbing his eyes and wondering if he should crash at his brother's place. His home wasn't far, but he felt like he didn't even have the energy to walk there. Maybe Kieran would let him sleep here at the table?

A hand on his arm made Sloan look up. Baxter was smiling at him, and he tilted his chin toward the door. "You could stay with me in the guest room tonight," he offered.

Sloan was pretty sure both Robin and Kieran were listening, but he didn't care. "I might accept that offer. I don't want to be without you tonight."

Baxter's smile widened. "I don't want to be without you, either. Come on. Let's go to bed."

Sloan nodded and staggered to his feet. Baxter took his hand and pulled, but not before snatching the bottle he'd left on the table. Sloan had eaten dinner earlier, so he wasn't hungry, but apparently, Baxter was, and it made Sloan think about Baxter possibly snacking on him.

Baxter had said it was something he only did when he was in a serious relationship, but Sloan wasn't sure that was what they had. He *wanted* their relationship to be serious, but for that to happen, they'd need time.

"So it's like that, huh?" Robin asked with a smile.

Baxter grinned. "Don't worry. We won't make noise. We're both too tired to do anything tonight." He winked. "Besides, we already had fun earlier."

Robin groaned. "Please don't talk about that. I don't want to imagine you and Sloan doing anything in the guest room."

"And with that, I'm going back to bed for a few hours," Kieran declared. "Get some rest. That's an order—for all of you." He paused. "But whatever *is* happening between you, I'm happy for you. It was about time you had some fun."

Sloan grimaced. "Thanks, but can we not talk about my sex life?"

Kieran laughed, and Sloan felt himself relax. Whatever

happened in the world outside, he and Kieran were family, and that would never stop.

All four of them shuffled out into the hallway, headed to their respective bedrooms. Before they could reach them, though, someone screamed.

Sloan and Baxter looked at each other. Then, they turned around as one and sprinted toward the door.

The scream couldn't mean anything good, and Baxter was terrified that he and Sloan had led the dragons straight to the pack. That didn't make sense, since they'd been dumping the bodies here, so the dragons already knew where the pack was, but fear wasn't rational. The pack and some of its members had come to mean a lot to Baxter, and he'd hate it if something were to happen to them.

"Where did the scream come from?" Robin asked.

Robin and Kieran hadn't stayed behind, but then Baxter hadn't expected them to. They were the guys in charge of this pack, and it was their responsibility and duty to find out what had happened.

"The edge of the forest by Ollis's house," Sloan said. "Look. Something is moving between the trees."

Baxter wasn't sure which house Sloan was talking about, but he looked in the same direction as the others, and, sure enough, something was moving between the trees. He couldn't tell what it was from here, at least not until the figure came running out of the woods.

"Dammit. That's Michael," Sloan said.

Baxter put on a burst of speed and reached the man first. He was young, probably in his early twenties, if even that, and he looked terrified.

"What happened?" Baxter asked as he stopped next to Michael.

The wolf stared at him without saying anything. Baxter didn't want to scare him, but he needed answers.

"Michael!" Sloan said as he reached them.

"They're in the woods," Michael answered.

"Who is?"

"Anthony and Eleanor." Sloan grabbed both of Michael's shoulders and gave him a firm shake. "Focus. Tell me what's going on," he ordered.

Michael licked his lips. "We went into the woods because Eleanor thought we could find another body. We were poking around when these guys came out from between the trees. They attacked us, and Anthony told me to run when Eleanor was wounded. I should have stayed with them."

Kieran and Robin had already disappeared between the trees, and while Baxter wanted to stay with Sloan, he went after them. He'd be more useful defending the pack than hanging around and trying to comfort Michael.

His heart would have raced if he'd still been alive, like always when he went on missions. That was one more thing he would miss when he quit. There was nothing quite like knowing you were throwing yourself into danger and might not come out of it intact, and it gave him the impression that he was still alive.

He'd find other ways to make that happen.

When the scent of blood hit his nose, he knew which way to go. He also knew Robin had probably smelled it, too, so he wasn't surprised to find him in the thick of things when he reached the sound of fighting he'd started hearing a few seconds before.

He took a moment to look around and evaluate the situation. A girl was sitting with her back against a tree, her arm held against her chest. Her eyes were wide and full of tears, and she didn't seem to be able to look away from the fighting. A man stood in front of her, half crouched in a defensive position, ready to act if someone attacked her. The people who'd wounded her were too busy to do that, though. Both Kieran and Robin were fighting three guys simultaneously, and Baxter thought he recognized one of the hunters he'd seen in that building when he and his team asked them about the drugs.

Dammit. They should have known better than to let the hunters go free.

Baxter threw himself into the mix. Since Robin had training and could deal with all three guys simultaneously, Baxter went to Kieran, hoping to help him. Kieran gave him a grateful smile, and Baxter knew he'd made the right decision.

When one of the guys tried to punch Kieran, Baxter put himself in his path and grabbed his wrist. He pulled, raising his knee at the same time, and nailed the hunter in the groin. It wasn't enough to put him down, but he folded in half, and Baxter took the opportunity to grab a second hunter by the shirt and pull him away from Kieran.

A howl in the forest made him freeze.

He expected Sloan to come running from between the trees in his wolf form, but when he arrived, he was human. He wasn't alone. A small group of four wolves had come with him, and even though they were clearly hesitant, they threw themselves into the fight. They stuck in groups of two, nipping at the hunters' heels, jumping on their backs when they had the opportunity. One of the hunters was flat on the ground, and the wolf who'd done it sat on his back and snarled at him when he tried to get back to his feet.

Hunters didn't usually hurt wolves. Baxter supposed they were here because they knew two vampires were with the pack, but they didn't know what they were facing. They had no idea how to deal with fangs and claws, and it showed.

More hunters came from between the trees, but Baxter was more hopeful now. Obviously, some of the pack members had decided to step in and help their alpha and their beta protect the pack, and they needed all the help they could get. Robin and Baxter might be trained for this, but it didn't mean they could take on all the hunters by themselves.

Someone jumped on Baxter's back and wrapped their arm around his throat. If he'd been human, the hold might have suffocated him, but instead, he grabbed the arm, leaned forward, and pulled. The hunter went flying over Baxter's head and landed in front of him. Baxter was still holding the guy's arm, and he quickly twisted, landing on the guy's stomach. A few punches and the hunter was out like a light.

Baxter got back to his feet and looked around to check who needed help. His heart dropped when he saw that Sloan was in trouble fighting three hunters at once. He was bleeding from his thigh, but that hadn't stopped him. Baxter suspected not much would.

He rushed toward Sloan. When one of the hunters tried to attack, Baxter grabbed him and pulled him back, kicking his feet from under him. He slammed his knee into the hunter's stomach and punched him in the face, snarling for good measure.

"Thanks," Sloan said.

He sounded out of breath, and Baxter had to remember that the pack wasn't trained to deal with this kind of attack. It was a miracle they were all still standing, but he and Robin needed to put an end to this.

He got back to his feet and put his back to Sloan's. "Which one hurt you? I'm going to kick his ass."

Sloan chuckled even as he ducked to avoid a punch aimed at his head. Baxter grabbed the hunter's arm and pulled, then punched the hunter before slamming him against a tree.

"You just knocked him out," Sloan said.

Baxter had knocked out several hunters, but he still looked around and tried to identify the one who'd hurt Sloan. If they needed to torture some of them to get answers, he'd pick that one.

Baxter was trying not to kill the hunters. He didn't want to create new vampires, especially when these vampires would hate the people they now belonged with. Sometimes, though, it was unavoidable. If he had to kill to defend Sloan, he hoped Sloan wouldn't look at him differently.

He slammed the head of the hunter he was fighting with against the nearest tree and let the body fall to the ground. When he turned, Sloan was grappling with a hunter who was holding a knife. He didn't seem to be able to push the man away, so Baxter stepped in.

He grabbed the hunter, who was trying to stab Sloan, and pulled him close, tearing into his throat. He didn't drink, not wanting to taste the hunter's blood. It wasn't dirty, and it didn't taste different from any human's blood, but it didn't feel right considering the circumstances. The body dropped, and Baxter found himself face to face with Sloan.

Sloan's eyes were wide, and Baxter realized he was staring at his mouth. Since he'd just killed a man using his fangs, he knew what he looked like. He hoped he wasn't scaring Sloan, but even if he was, he wouldn't change it.

This was who he was. He was an enforcer, a protector, and a vampire. If Sloan couldn't accept him like this, then maybe they shouldn't be together.

Sloan wasn't afraid of Baxter, even the way he looked now, his fangs dripping blood. He was seeing Baxter in a light he'd never seen him in, and he wasn't quite sure what to think of it. Baxter had killed a man to save him, and the thought that he cared about him so much made Sloan's heart race.

Baxter grimaced. "You're afraid of me."

Sloan reached for him. Now wasn't the time or the place,

but he didn't want Baxter to think that. He grabbed Baxter's hand and squeezed. "I'm not. Thank you. I think he'd have managed to stab me if you hadn't intervened."

Baxter still looked hesitant, but he nodded.

The fight was winding down, for which Sloan was thankful. He'd never been in this kind of situation, and he hoped he never would be again. Their pack had always been peaceful, even when his father had pushed the other alphas in the area to the end of their patience. No one had wanted to start a war, but these people didn't seem to care about that.

Now, Baxter took it upon himself to protect Sloan. He punched and kicked and killed one more hunter. When that hunter's body hit the ground, the forest went silent.

Sloan looked around. There had been more hunters than he'd expected or had seen in the beginning. He counted eleven on the ground now, most of them bleeding, but not all of them dead. One was whimpering, sitting with his back against the tree and trying to scramble away. Another was still under the wolf who had put him down earlier, trying to buck it off him. It wasn't working, though. Ollis was pissed, and he wasn't going anywhere.

Both Kieran and Robin were still standing. Anthony and Eleanor were huddled together, their backs against a tree. Sloan had been surprised when Michael had decided to come with him, and he wasn't the only one. By the time Sloan had managed to calm Michael enough, Ollis and two of his friends had reached them. Sloan had told them to stay back, but they hadn't listened, and he hadn't insisted. If they wanted to fight to protect the pack, they should be allowed to.

The wolves shifted back to their human form and high-fived. Sloan rolled his eyes. Even though Ollis and his friends were in their late twenties, sometimes, they behaved like kids.

A noise from the woods made him turn around, ready to continue defending the pack. He didn't have to, though. More pack members started to arrive, looking ready to fight if they had to. They were a little late, although he didn't miss the way his elderly neighbor kicked one of the hunters in the leg as she passed by.

"What are you doing here?" Kieran asked. There was a streak of blood on his cheek, but he didn't seem to be wounded.

"We want to help," Mike said. He'd always been on the side of Kieran and Sloan's father, so Sloan was surprised to see him there.

"What do you mean?" Kieran said warily.

"This pack is our home. It's our duty and honor to defend it, and that's why we're here."

"What about my father?"

Mike hesitated and looked around. He wasn't the only one present who'd supported Kieran and Sloan's father, but they seemed to have elected him as their mouthpiece.

"You're not the perfect alpha, but you're trying, and you're doing everything you can," Mike eventually said. "You're young, but you'll learn. We want the pack to give you that opportunity, and that won't happen if we continue being stubborn and supporting your father. I apologize. I shouldn't have, Alpha."

Sloan had no idea what happened, but if this was the result of having the pack attacked, then maybe it wasn't a bad thing. From what he could see, no pack member was wounded too badly, which certainly looked like a win to him.

Kieran nodded. "Don't worry about it. If you truly want to help, you can take care of the bodies. I know it's not a great job, but it needs to be done."

"Of course." Mike gestured, and several wolves stepped forward.

Sloan had expected someone to protest or at least grumble, but no one did. Instead, they went to work, pulling the bodies away, and Sloan could only look, amazed at what was happening.

"Ollis, can you and your friend grab the few who are still alive and put them together?" Kieran asked.

He was in charge, just like an alpha would be. Sloan had always known that his brother would be great in time of need, and he hadn't been wrong.

But Sloan was the beta, which meant he had authority, too. He waved at Michael to come closer. The young man had shifted back to his human form, and he was shivering, but his jaw was set in a stubborn expression.

"Beta?" he asked when he reached Sloan.

"I want you and Anthony to take Eleanor home. Make sure she's okay, and if she's not, get the healer."

Michael nodded and rushed to his friends. Now that the only badly wounded person had been taken care of, Sloan and the others could focus on getting answers from the hunters. Sloan had recognized one of them as the leader Baxter and his team had talked to, and he wanted to pound the guy into the ground.

"You're wounded," Baxter said before Sloan could reach the asshole.

The pain chose that moment to flare. Sloan looked down at his thigh, where that guy with the knife had stabbed him. "It's fine. It's not deep."

Baxter arched a brow. "And you know that because you've been stabbed more than once?"

"I'll be fine."

"Both Robin and I have some training. We can patch you up until the healer can see you."

"Let them fuss over you," Kieran ordered. "We won't start the interrogation until they're done. I want to get everyone away from here first anyway."

Sloan and Kieran exchanged a glance. What the pack had

done was amazing. Not every single pack member was here, but that was understandable. Some of them had families and children, and they'd stayed back. But all the people who'd been going along with what Sloan and Kieran's father was doing were present, which meant they'd finally accepted Kieran as their alpha. The mood of the pack had shifted, and as they gathered the bodies, they seemed excited to be working together and protecting their pack. The hunters had been defeated, and they took that as a pack victory, as they should.

As Kieran had ordered, Sloan allowed Robin and Baxter to fuss over the wound in his thigh. It really wasn't bad, but his chest squeezed at the sight of Baxter taking care of him. He wanted more of this. He could do without the hunters and the stab wound, but he wanted Baxter to fuss over him for the rest of his life. Maybe it was too soon, or maybe not. Sloan didn't really care what other people would think. He only cared about Baxter and what he wanted.

"I'll take a better look at it once we're back home," Baxter said as he got to his feet. Sloan had needed to sit on the ground, since they were poking and it hurt, but Baxter offered his hand, and Sloan took it and allowed him to haul him to his feet.

"Home?"

Baxter shrugged and looked away. "You know. Your house."

And Baxter had called it home. Hopefully, one day, it *would* become his home.

By the time Robin and Baxter were done, all the bodies had disappeared. Sloan had heard Kieran give Mike quick instructions on how to deal with them. They couldn't just bury the bodies, because these hunters were dhampirs. They'd died a violent death, which meant they'd rise again as vampires if they weren't stopped. Kieran's orders had been to cut everyone's head off, and while Mike had paled when he'd heard it, he'd nodded and had looked determined. It was odd to trust him to do this job or anything else, but Sloan knew that none of them would have their head by the time the bodies were buried.

"It's almost dawn," Baxter said.

"You and Baxter should head home. Kieran and I will take care of the last hunters."

Baxter shook his head, just like Sloan had expected him to. "I'm not going anywhere until I have answers."

So the four of them gathered around Peter. He was the hunter Ollis had sat on during most of the fight, and he looked pissed. Someone had tied him up, though, so he wasn't going anywhere.

"This is all your fault," he spat out.

Sloan was confused. "What's our fault?"

Peter's entire body trembled with rage. "They're dying."

"Stop talking as if we understand what you're saying and explain yourself," Kieran ordered.

"The hunters. They're dying because of those drugs. This is all your fault."

None of this made sense. "Shifters are dying because of the drugs, too. As are vampires. Why are you saying it's our fault?" he asked.

"You're the one making those drugs."

"We're not. We wouldn't be dying because of it if we were." But considering those drugs killed vampires and shifters, Sloan could too easily imagine the ravage they did on a human body. Until they died a violent death, dhampirs were nothing more than human.

"This is all your fault," Peter insisted.

Sloan sighed. They wouldn't get any more answers from Peter. From what Sloan understood, Peter had been losing hunters, and he'd decided it was the pack's fault. He'd attacked, and he'd lost.

"I'll take care of him and the others," Robin murmured. "The rest of you, go home."

"I'm staying," Kieran declared.

Robin stared at him for a moment before nodding. "We'll do this together. Sloan, Baxter, go home. We'll be fine."

Sloan wanted to stay, too, but his alpha mate had given him an order, and he understood why Robin and Kieran wanted to do this on their own. He took Baxter's hand and pulled him along, and, together, they walked back to Kieran's house.

It looked like they'd end up sleeping in Baxter's guestroom, after all.

CHAPTER SIX

It had been a week, and Baxter was getting antsy. He'd expected the dragons to do something, maybe attack the pack or try to contact them, but they hadn't. They hadn't done *anything* except stay away, and Baxter didn't know what it meant. From what little he knew about dragons, it couldn't be anything good, but that didn't help.

He was supposed to go back to work soon. Actually, he'd been expected back to work last week, but Oren had wanted him to stick around, and he'd been more than happy to say yes. He still planned to quit his job, but not yet, not when the pack was in danger. He'd never forgive himself if he could have done something and hadn't been able to because he wasn't an enforcer anymore.

So here he was, still an enforcer, still somehow on vacation. Being in this limbo didn't help, but Baxter wouldn't step back. He was doing everything he could to keep the pack safe, and he could think about his future later.

He still didn't know what he'd do once all of this was over. He'd told Oren he was quitting, and Oren hadn't tried to change his mind, but after that? Baxter had no idea. He wanted to come back to the pack, but he didn't know if he'd be allowed to. He was here on vacation, but no one ever talked about him moving in permanently.

But things had changed since that attack. Most pack members had relaxed around him, and now he felt like he was part of their family. They said hello, talked to him, and had stopped acting as if he was going to snack on them if he got a bit hungry. That didn't mean they wanted him to become a pack member, but it was something he'd started thinking about, and he had more hope than he'd had in the beginning.

"I've had enough," Robin declared.

Baxter blinked and looked up from his bottle of blood. He, Robin, Sloan, and Kieran were sitting at Kieran and Robin's kitchen table. The two wolves were eating dinner while Robin and Baxter were drinking blood. They'd become even closer after the attack, and Baxter enjoyed these moments. It was like he'd found a family again, but then, he'd never really lost the rest of his team. This was just different, and he couldn't say he disliked it. If anything, he enjoyed it, and it gave him a look into what his future might be if he stuck around.

"What are you talking about?" Kieran asked. He reached for Robin, taking his hand and squeezing.

Robin smiled at him, but he wasn't done. "All of this. I'm done sitting around and waiting for something to happen. It's killing me."

"You know what Oren said. You can't go looking for the dragons."

"I know what he said, but I'm not one of his team members anymore. I don't have to obey his orders, and I don't think waiting is helping. We can only imagine what the dragons are doing and planning right now, and I don't want the pack to be so vulnerable. No, we have to do something."

Baxter agreed, but he was technically still an enforcer. Oren had told him to stay put, and he should do that.

But he wouldn't be an enforcer for long. What could Oren do if he disobeyed? Fire him? It was already too late for that, and Robin was right. Waiting wasn't helping anyone, least of all the pack. Everyone was nervous. They knew they could defend themselves from the group of hunters, but dragons would be very different.

Kieran and Robin had told the pack what they knew about

the dragons because they felt they had to, but now everyone kept staring at the sky. That *really* wasn't helping. If anything, it was making things worse, and Baxter agreed they needed to do something.

"We're not doing anything," Kieran said. He pulled Robin closer, and Robin leaned against his side, allowing him to wrap his arm around his shoulders and kiss his temple.

"This is driving me nuts," Robin murmured. "I can't just sit around and wait to see what happens."

Sloan cleared his throat. "Maybe we could go out? Take some time away from the pack and its problems and have fun."

That was actually a good idea. Sticking around the pack wasn't helping, and everyone was frustrated. Baxter knew Robin, and when he was like that, there was a serious risk he'd do something stupid if he didn't distract himself. Baxter might, too. He'd just been thinking about disobeying Oren's orders, after all.

"What did you have in mind?" Kieran asked.

"Well, there are a few supernatural clubs around. Maybe we could go to one of them? Although not to Midnight."

"Will vampires be welcome?" Baxter asked.

Sloan smiled at him. "I wouldn't want to go anywhere you couldn't follow."

Baxter resisted the urge to kiss him for only a few seconds. Then he remembered he could and that Kieran and Robin didn't care that he and Sloan were sleeping together. He turned in his seat, grabbed Sloan's face with both his hands, and pulled him close. Sloan laughed as Baxter kissed him, but the sound quickly faded, and Sloan kissed him back.

"Enough of that at the table," Kieran said after a moment.

He sounded amused, and he chuckled when Baxter glared at him.

"I think it's a good idea," Kieran continued, smirking.

"We've been obsessing over the dragons and how to keep the pack safe, and it hasn't been helping any of us. Maybe an evening of distraction will help."

"What if something happens while we're not here?" Robin asked.

"Nothing will. If it does, though, we'll come back. We won't be going far."

Robin slowly nodded. He didn't look convinced, but Kieran would change his mind. As far as Baxter had seen, he always did.

Getting ready to leave took them a bit longer than Baxter was used to. Since both the alpha and the beta would be away, they needed to put someone else in charge. Baxter wasn't surprised when Kieran chose Ollis. He'd been of great help when the hunters had attacked, and he'd been around Kieran's house several times since then. It was good to see that Kieran and Robin had found people in the pack they trusted beyond Sloan.

Then they were on their way. They took only one car, which meant Baxter and Sloan could cuddle in the backseat. Baxter took full advantage of that, wrapping himself around Sloan like an octopus. Sloan didn't seem to mind. If anything, he looked amused, and he acted like he couldn't keep away from Baxter. He was always touching and kissing him, and Baxter loved it.

It was hard not to dream and make plans when they were like this. Sloan wanted Baxter, and Baxter wanted Sloan, but would it be a good idea for Baxter to move here? Of course he'd have to ask Kieran and Robin, and maybe that was the first thing he should do. He didn't want to give Sloan false hope, just in case.

But what if Kieran and Robin said no if he asked to move in with the pack? Baxter didn't have to be a full-fledged pack member. He wasn't a wolf, so being a pack member didn't mean as much to him as it did to shifters. Maybe having him around without being a pack member would be easier on everyone, or maybe not. Baxter had spent several weeks here, but it still wasn't enough for him to really know shifters and these wolves in particular.

Or maybe he should talk to Sloan first. Maybe Sloan could help him convince Kieran and Robin he should be allowed to stay. And if they couldn't, well, Baxter supposed he could always stay in town. The town didn't belong to the pack, so no one could forbid him from doing that.

But Baxter had made his decision. If he was allowed, he'd stay with the pack, or at the very least, in town. He wanted to see where the relationship he was building with Sloan was going and whether it had a future. If it didn't, he'd leave. If it did, though, he wouldn't be going anywhere. It didn't matter if he became a pack member or not. Sloan was it for him, and he'd do everything he could to keep him in his life.

Clubs weren't Sloan's thing. He wasn't crazy about crowds, the overwhelming scents, and the noise. He had to admit it was easier to lose himself in a crowd than doing so at home, though.

He followed the others into the club Kieran had chosen. Music made the walls vibrate, and having so many people in the same room meant it was freaking hot. It also meant Baxter was plastered against Sloan's front as they tried to navigate their way to a table.

That was one thing Sloan didn't mind about crowds.

No matter how much he disliked clubs, he was happy to have the opportunity to spend time with his brother, Robin, and even more with Baxter. They still hadn't talked about whether or not Baxter would stay once this mess was over, but Sloan was tempted to do so more every day. He was just terrified of the answer Baxter would give him.

What if Baxter had no intention of staying? What he and Sloan shared felt real and important, but maybe Sloan was the only one to feel that way. Maybe for Baxter, this was only a fling, and he'd forget all about Sloan as soon as he was gone.

Or maybe he was as in love with Sloan as Sloan was with him, and Sloan just needed to find his courage and ask him. It wasn't like he'd find out any other way.

He was relieved when Kieran finally found a booth, and the four of them slid on the benches around it. He didn't miss the way Robin and Baxter made sure he and Kieran were on the inside of the booth, but he didn't say anything about it. The two of them had been enforcers for a long time, and they couldn't just forget their training.

"What now?" he asked.

Baxter beamed. "Clubs really aren't your thing, are they?" he asked.

He shook his head, but Baxter was already pulling him out of the booth. Sloan went along with it because he trusted Baxter with everything he had, including his life. Baxter wiggled his fingers at Robin and Kieran, took Sloan's hand, and tugged him along.

Toward the dance floor.

The last time they'd been in this situation, Sloan had watched Baxter dance from afar. He'd had to resist the urge to pull the people who wanted to dance with him away and growl at them that the man was his. Now he didn't have to do any of that. As soon as they were on the dance floor, Baxter grabbed Sloan's hips and pulled him close, so close that their groins brushed together as they moved.

Sloan put his arms around Baxter's neck and went along with it.

Everyone around them would know who Sloan belonged to, and that was more than okay with him. It kept them away, which was perfect, in Sloan's opinion. He didn't care if they watched, but he didn't want anyone to try to talk to Baxter or touch him. He was possessive, and he knew it might become a problem, but things between him and Baxter were new. Sloan was terrified of losing him, and while that might be solved by talking to him, for now, it was time to dance.

So they did.

Baxter didn't even look at anyone else. His entire focus was on Sloan, and that helped soothe Sloan's fears.

Baxter's nails dug into Sloan's sides as he held him close while swaying against him. The movements, combined with the heat and Baxter's scent, made Sloan go hard in his jeans, but he doubted anyone would care even if they noticed. He was pretty sure the two guys in the corner were having full sex in plain sight of everyone. Who would care about an erection when that kind of show was happening?

So Sloan danced and thought. He was still tense, mostly because he wasn't used to having so many supernatural creatures around him. He seldom left pack territory, and when he did, it was to go into town. Most of the people were humans there, not supernatural creatures, although he was sure some of them lived in town. But it was no one he had regular contact with, and certainly not so many people at once.

But Baxter seemed comfortable, and that helped. The problem was that Sloan had a hard time not thinking about Baxter and their future. He wanted to ask Baxter what he was thinking of doing once he was done with his job, but would Baxter answer?

Would a small-town life be something Baxter wanted? He'd seemed to be having fun lately, but maybe it was because he was working this case. Maybe he'd realized he was too used to having something to do and that leaving the enforcers wasn't for him after all. Or maybe he'd leave the enforcers, but he'd also leave town.

The questions were driving Sloan bananas. He wasn't about to ask Baxter about their future here in the middle of the dance floor, so he pushed all those questions away and focused on Baxter.

There was a lot to focus on. They were still dancing, and Baxter was plastered against Sloan's body, his head thrown back, a wide smile on his face. He was loving this, and Sloan was ready to go out every night if it made Baxter happy. He doubted that would be the case from what he knew about Baxter, but it was good to see Baxter in a different situation. So far, they'd either been working or had been in pack territory. Sloan was seeing a new Baxter tonight, and he loved it.

Baxter looked at Sloan again, and his smile broadened. He pulled Sloan closer, and when he leaned forward, Sloan did, too. Their lips met, and Sloan lost himself in the kiss.

There was no way for him to know what the future would be like beyond asking, but for now, this was enough. He could feel how much Baxter cared for him through the kiss and in every movement Baxter made, and he never wanted to lose this.

Baxter's hands roamed on Sloan's body, and Sloan let him. He wasn't about to have sex like those two guys from earlier, but this he didn't mind. It felt as if Baxter was showing everyone that Sloan belonged to him, and Sloan wanted that. He wanted to belong to Baxter and for Baxter to belong to him.

They danced for ages, pressed together, their lips never far from each other's. A couple of guys tried to cut in, but Baxter shook his head every time. He only wanted to dance with Sloan, just like Sloan only wanted to dance with him.

"I'm thirsty," Baxter said after a while, leaning closer so Sloan could hear him.

"Let's grab a drink, then."

Since this was a bar geared toward supernatural creatures, they offered blood as well as other drinks and food. It wouldn't be a problem for Baxter to find something to drink, and Sloan could do with a bottle of water.

He looked around as Baxter pulled him toward the bar, trying to find Kieran and Robin. When he did, they were on the dance floor, slow dancing to a rhythm only they could hear. Their foreheads were pressed together, and Kieran was saying something that made Robin smile.

Sloan looked away. He felt like he was intruding by watching them, but he was happy for his brother. He'd found the perfect man, and Robin was giving Kieran everything Kieran deserved and had wanted for so many years. Taking their father's place hadn't been easy on him, but he wasn't facing it alone. He had Sloan, but even more importantly, he had Robin.

Sloan and Baxter reached the bar, and it only took a few moments for the bartender to come to them when Baxter waved. Baxter leaned over the bar, screaming their order so the bartender could hear him. She nodded and turned around to get the drinks ready, and Baxter turned his attention to Sloan.

Sloan pulled him into his arms and kissed him. It was as if he couldn't stop, and he didn't want to. He wanted to kiss Baxter forever, and he didn't care if it made him sound corny or sappy.

"We're going to talk once we're home," he whispered.

Baxter frowned. "Nothing bad, I hope?"

"Nothing bad." Sloan didn't want Baxter to be worried.

He kissed him again, but as he was about to lose himself in the kiss, something caught the corner of his eye. From where he was, he could see the bartender getting blood ready for Baxter in a stainless-steel glass after heating it. She dumped the blood from the container into the glass, but that wasn't all she put in it. She briefly looked around, and then something white dropped from her fingers into the glass. She had Sloan's water ready, so she grabbed both and brought them over.

Baxter smiled and took the glass, raising it to his lips, but Sloan grabbed his wrist before he could drink from it.

"What did you put in it?" he asked the bartender.

Her eyes widened. "I'm sorry?"

"I saw you. What did you put in his glass?"

She shook her head. "I don't know what you're talking about. I have work to do."

She moved away without even asking them to pay. That was enough to tell Sloan he hadn't imagined it, and he reached above the bar, grabbing her wrist and pulling her close.

"You're going to tell me what you put in my boyfriend's glass, and you're going to tell me now," he said with a growl, his wolf close to the surface.

He'd get answers, even if he had to kill her.

Baxter hadn't seen anything, but if Sloan said the bartender had put something in his drink, then she had. He trusted Sloan implicitly, and he was lucky that Sloan had been there with him when this happened. If he hadn't been, Baxter would have drunk it, and who knew what would have happened to him.

His stomach felt like lead. Most drugs didn't have an effect on vampires, which meant that whatever the bartender had tried giving him, she knew it would. It wouldn't have made sense for her to do this otherwise. There was only one drug Baxter could think of that could do something to him, though, and the thought that she'd been trying to give him the drugs that had killed so many vampires and supernatural creatures made him feel sick. Why would she do that? None of it made sense, but Baxter *would* get answers.

The people around them were starting to notice something

was wrong. When a tall guy strode in their direction, his expression thunderous, Baxter put himself into his path.

"What the fuck do you think you're doing?" the guy asked.

Baxter was glad he'd thought about grabbing his enforcer badge when he'd left the house. "I'm a council enforcer," he said, digging it out of his pocket. "We need to talk to the bartender, and possibly the owner of this place."

The guy looked from Baxter's badge to the bartender.

She was still behind the bar, and Sloan was still pulling on her wrist. He looked pissed, and Baxter hoped he wouldn't do something stupid. They wouldn't get answers if he killed her, but he'd end up in trouble if he did. It wouldn't be self-defense, not when she hadn't hurt him.

"I'm the owner," the tall guy said. "Arlen."

Baxter nodded. "My name is Baxter, and this is Sloan."

Arlen gestured. "Follow me. You, too, Leanne."

The bartender looked terrified, but Baxter couldn't tell if it was because of Sloan or Arlen.

He didn't care.

Sloan didn't seem to, either, because he pulled her from behind the bar, dragging her along when Arlen started walking away. She put up a fight, but no one tried to intervene on her behalf. The crowd parted for Arlen, a sure sign that everyone knew who he was. Thankfully, it caught Kieran and Robin's attention, and they followed.

Arlen disappeared down a hallway Baxter had noticed earlier, and when Baxter stepped inside, he saw several doors. All of them were closed, but he wasn't surprised when Arlen stopped in front of one that said *no entrance*. Arlen unlocked the door, then pushed it open and stepped inside.

Baxter and the others followed. Leanne tried to pull away, but Sloan growled at her, and she squeaked and stopped moving. He looked like he might eat her if she tried running away, and while Baxter knew he'd never do something like that, Leanne didn't. She was understandably terrified, but Baxter couldn't find it in himself to care. She might have just tried to kill him, and he didn't look kindly on that.

Arlen didn't say anything about Kieran and Robin being there. He closed the door behind them and gestured at the chairs in front of the desk. "Sit down."

Kieran and Robin did, but Sloan kept his grip on Leanne, and Baxter had too much energy to want to sit.

Arlen walked around the desk and sat behind it. Now that the light was more natural, Baxter took a better look at him.

He was a good-looking guy. His hair was dark and long in a way that made him look like he'd just hopped out of bed. His jaw was square and set in a tight expression, but that wasn't what caught Baxter's attention. No, it was the eyes — because they were red.

It wasn't a bright red, but rather, a muted one that people wouldn't even notice in the darkness of the club. They weren't in the club anymore, though. They were in an office, and it was easy for them to see the color.

Baxter and Robin exchanged a glance. Baxter couldn't remember ever seeing a creature with red eyes, and it worried him. What kind of creature was Arlen? More importantly, what kind of person was he?

"Care to tell me what's going on?" Arlen asked.

"I don't know what's happening," Leanne said. "I got them their drinks, and this guy started saying I put something in the blood."

Arlen looked at her. Leanne snapped her mouth shut so quickly that Baxter heard her teeth click together.

Arlen seemed satisfied and looked at Baxter. "Is it true?"

"Sloan did say she dropped something in my drink."

"I said that because she did," Sloan intervened. "I *saw* her drop something white into the blood."

And luckily, Baxter had grabbed the glass as they left the

bar. He wasn't quite sure how they were supposed to find out something had been dropped inside it, though. He held up the glass, but he had no intention of drinking the blood. "We could have this analyzed if you want proof."

Arlen waved him closer. "Just give it to me."

Baxter wasn't sure what Arlen was going to do with it, but he obeyed, placing the glass on the desk in front of him. He hoped Arlen wasn't about to throw everything away and act as if nothing had happened.

Instead of doing that, Arlen picked up the glass and sniffed it. His nose twitched, then, to Baxter's horror, he took a sip. Baxter was pretty sure Arlen wasn't a vampire, so why was he drinking blood?

Arlen grimaced. "There's definitely something in there, and I know what it is." He looked at Leanne. "How dare you do something like this?"

"I didn't do anything. As far as I know, he was the one to put something in the guy's drink," she protested.

Sloan looked like he was seconds away from shaking her, but Arlen put up a hand. "This is easily disproved," he said. He turned to his computer. "Leanne should have remembered that I have cameras all over the place," he said.

Baxter hadn't thought it possible, but Leanne turned even paler. She staggered, and Baxter suspected that only Sloan's hold on her kept her on her feet. He also thought that if Sloan hadn't been so angry, he'd have allowed her to drop to the floor.

Arlen typed on his keyboard, and everyone waited. Baxter and Robin looked at each other again, but Baxter didn't want to say anything in front of people he didn't trust. So far, Arlen was doing everything right, but it might not last. What would happen when he found proof that his bartender had tried to drug Baxter? And what did he mean when he'd said he knew what was in the blood? He'd looked horrified, which was enough to tell Baxter that whatever was happening wasn't good.

Arlen turned his computer screen so that Baxter and the others could see it. He clicked a few things on the screen, and a window opened. Baxter recognized the club. That camera was aimed toward the bar, and when Arlen zoomed, Baxter saw Leanne. He watched as he and Sloan approached the bar, and he spoke to Leanne. She stepped away to get their drinks ready, and he kissed Sloan. Sloan kissed him back, but his body went rigid after only a few moments, and Baxter looked from Sloan to Leanne.

Arlen backtracked the video, zoomed in on Leanne even more, and all of them watched her drop something small and white into the blood she then gave Baxter.

Arlen sat back in his chair. "What do you have to say for yourself?" he asked Leanne.

She stared at him as if she didn't understand the question. There was no denying that she'd tried drugging Baxter, though, and even though he had no proof, Baxter could imagine what drug she'd been trying to give him.

If Sloan hadn't been there, he'd probably have died. He didn't owe just his happiness to Sloan, but also his life.

Sloan was pissed, but killing Leanne wouldn't help. Besides, he'd never killed anyone in his life. He didn't want to start now, even though Baxter's life had been in danger.

He had to remind himself that Baxter was fine. Sloan had seen everything, and he'd made sure Baxter didn't drink the blood. Nothing would happen to him, so why was Sloan's heart still racing? Why was he still terrified to look away from Leanne in case she tried attacking Baxter?

"Leanne?" Arlen prodded.

She tried to jerk her arm away from Sloan, and this time,

Sloan let her. It was getting harder for him not to slam her against the wall and snarl at her, and he didn't want to do anything he'd regret later. He'd wanted to keep Baxter safe, and Baxter was. There was nothing else Sloan could do.

"You know what I did and why I did it," Leanne snarled. "You're a traitor to our race, and you shouldn't be allowed to live."

Sloan blinked. He had no idea what was going on, but it didn't sound good. It also sounded like Arlen had his own problems, and Sloan felt kind of sorry for him. Whatever he'd done, it couldn't be easy to be considered a traitor of his race.

Arlen slammed his hands on his desk, making all of them jump. "I'm a traitor because I don't want to kill people?" he asked.

Leanne set her jaw. "You know you are. We've all decided we would do this, but you're not helping. You don't care about any of this."

"I'm not about to kill innocent people just because I was ordered to." He looked at Baxter. "I'm sorry for what happened."

Baxter shrugged. "I'm fine, but I have to say I'm curious about what's going on here."

He wasn't the only one. Sloan had a lot of questions, and he wanted answers. He wasn't sure he'd get them, but it wouldn't stop him from trying.

"I'll give you answers as soon as I'm done dealing with Leanne." Arlen grabbed his phone and dialed a number from memory. "Merrick? I need you in my office, now."

That was all Arlen said. He hung up once he was done talking and put his phone down.

Leanne stepped toward the desk. "What are you going to do? You can't hurt me. You know I was doing this for the clan."

Arlen glared at her, and it was enough for her to snap her

mouth shut and step back. Only seconds later, someone knocked on the door. Arlen got up to open, and another man came in.

This had to be Merrick, although Sloan had no idea who Merrick was. He was a tall man, with light brown hair cut short and blue eyes. Where Arlen was slight and had long limbs, Merrick's shoulders were broad and heavily muscled. His t-shirt shifted as he moved, the muscles bulging under it.

"You needed me?" he asked.

Arlen nodded. "Leanne was caught dropping something into a customer's drink. Take her to the back room and lock her in. I'll deal with her later."

Sloan was tempted to ask what *dealing with her* meant, but he doubted he'd like the answer. Something was happening that he didn't understand, and he didn't want to make any judgment calls before he knew everything.

Merrick didn't protest or say anything. He grabbed Leanne's arm and pulled her into the hallway, ignoring her screams of protest. She was putting up a fight, but it didn't seem to do anything to Merrick.

Arlen closed the door behind them and walked back to his chair behind the desk. He sat down in it, and his shoulders slumped.

"I'm really sorry about all of this. It should never have happened."

"But it did," Sloan said.

"I'd like to put my superior on a conference call with us," Baxter said. "Something tells me he needs to know what's going on, too."

Arlen nodded. "Feel free. At least this way, I'll only have to say this once."

Sloan thought that Arlen should repeat the story as many times as he needed, but he didn't say it out loud. He could tell Arlen was a supernatural creature, but he had no idea what kind, and it made him wary.

It only took Baxter a few moments to put Oren on a conference call and explain what had happened. Then they all listened.

"Once again, I'd like to apologize for what my bartender did," Arlen started. "I didn't think she'd do something like this, or I wouldn't have hired her."

"Just get to the point," Sloan muttered.

Arlen shot him an amused glance, but he nodded. "Of course. I apologize again. What Leanne was attempting to give your boyfriend is a drug we created. It was created specifically for vampires, though it also works on other supernatural creatures. She intended to kill your boyfriend."

Sloan swallowed. He'd imagined this was what was happening, but hearing it made him feel sick. "You created this drug?"

Arlen shook his head. "What I meant when I said that we created it was, my people did so."

Sloan swallowed. "You're a dragon shifter."

Arlen smiled. It wasn't unkind, and it didn't make Sloan feel afraid. That didn't mean he didn't have to be wary of Arlen, though.

"I am, as are Leanne and Merrick. I should have known better than to hire her when she came to me and said she left the clan."

"Can you start from the beginning?" Oren asked.

Arlen sighed and linked his fingers together on top of his stomach. "You have to understand this isn't something we tell anyone. Dragon shifters are extremely secretive, and I'm no different. I don't want to tell you about this, but I realize that the time has come to take a stance."

Sloan wanted to shake him to get the words out of him faster, but knowing that Arlen could kill him with one move made him stay where he was. Baxter seemed to understand what Sloan was going through, and he leaned closer, as if lending him his support. Sloan grabbed his hand and squeezed, unwilling to let go.

"There've always been dragon shifters around," Arlen said. "We live in clans, some extremely small, others bigger. I was part of the biggest clan in the area until recently. Dragons keep to themselves, but sometimes, some of us want more. A lot of dragons believe they're superior to other kinds of shifters and, of course, humans."

"And vampires," Baxter murmured.

Arlen nodded. "It's bullshit, but some people truly believe it, and apparently, Leanne is one of those people. My clan is behind these drugs. I didn't know anything about it until recently. But when people started dying around the club, I went to my clan leader. He told me what he'd been planning, from the drugs to giving them to vampires and shifters and waiting for them to kill each other. He thought it was a great plan because it meant dragons wouldn't get their hands dirty."

"Except you have," Robin pointed out. "Even though you're not killing vampires and shifters with your own hands, you're still killing them with drugs."

Arlen nodded. "I tried to stop this, but I'm not powerful enough to do it. In the end, Merrick and I left the clan. We wanted nothing to do with what was happening, and we still don't."

"Why do they want us to kill each other?" Kieran asked. "Why did they target my pack?"

Arlen's eyes widened. "You're the alpha of the wolf pack in town?"

Kieran nodded. "I am. Robin is my alpha mate, and Sloan is my beta."

Arlen's gaze drifted to Baxter, who rubbed the back of his neck and chuckled. "I'm just a council enforcer," he said deprecatingly.

Sloan wrapped an arm around Baxter's waist and pulled him even closer. "He's my boyfriend."

"I have to say, I didn't expect vampires and wolf shifters to mingle this way."

"It looks like you didn't expect a lot of things," Sloan said through gritted teeth.

Arlen's smile fell. "You're right. I was unable to do any-thing about the drugs because I'm only one man, but maybe we could ally. None of us can take the clan on our own, but together, we might have a chance."

And they'd have a war on their hands. Unfortunately, it didn't look like there was anything they could do against that. The dragons had been the ones to start this war, and the wolves and vampires would have to end it.

CHAPTER SEVEN

It was time to make the phone call. There was nothing else Baxter could do as a council enforcer, and he needed to call Oren and tell him he was quitting. He still didn't know what he'd do with his life, but this was the one thing he was sure of.

He took his phone out of his pocket and stared at the screen. Even though he'd made his decision and was convinced of it, it was still hard. The enforcers and his team had been his life for the past two decades. He'd feel lost without them and without being able to see his team members every day, but he knew he was making the right decision.

"Baxter?" Sloan called out.

Baxter lowered his phone. He stayed where he was, waiting for Sloan to find him.

When Sloan did, he smiled.

Baxter had moved in with Sloan. It wasn't official, and he hadn't moved a lot of things since he only had a few bags with him, but he was now staying with him rather than with Kieran and Robin. No one in the pack had said anything about it, but Baxter wasn't sure what that meant. He wanted to find out, but he was too afraid to ask.

"What are you doing here?" Sloan asked as he sat on the couch next to Baxter.

Baxter bit his lower lip. Maybe he should ask Sloan if he could stay before he quit. He'd still quit his job if Sloan said no, but at least he'd know what he was in for.

"I was about to call Oren."

"You think he heard anything else about the dragons?"

Baxter shrugged. "I don't know." After the talk they'd had with Arlen, things had slowed down. Most people in the area knew about the drugs now, so they were careful not to take them. That meant fewer people died, and the pack hadn't found any more bodies.

Baxter wasn't sure if it was because of Arlen or because people were more careful, but it didn't matter. The dragons were still a problem, but it wasn't a problem they could solve quickly. They'd kept in contact with Arlen, but he wasn't part of the clan anymore. He couldn't tell them much, although he'd been working with Oren and the team.

"I wanted to ask you something," Baxter said.

"I'm listening."

"I made my decision about whether or not I want to continue being an enforcer. I'm about to call Oren to tell him I quit."

Sloan smiled softly. "As long as you're sure it's what you want."

"I am. I want to find another way to help people."

"What do you want to ask me?"

Baxter swallowed. This was it. "Well, now that I'm not an enforcer anymore, I'm not sure what to do or where to go. I was wondering if maybe I could stay here? I know you're not the one who makes that kind of decision and that I have to ask Kieran, and I will, but I wanted to know what you thought about it first."

Sloan grabbed Baxter and pulled him into his arms. "Of course you can stay. And you don't have to ask Kieran. I'm allowing you to stay, and I'm the beta. It has to count for something."

Baxter laughed and hugged Sloan back. "I still want to talk to him."

"Whenever you want. He's not going to say no, Baxter.

You've become a friend to him, and Robin is happy to have you around. Besides, you've been helping and working your ass off, even though you were on vacation." Sloan rubbed his face. "And there's also the fact that you and Robin are trained, and we might need you with the dragons."

That wasn't why Baxter wanted to stay, but he'd be happy to defend the pack if he had to.

Knowing that he had a new home and wouldn't have to leave Sloan behind helped when he finally made the call to Oren. Sloan was with him, holding his free hand and smiling encouragingly. Baxter still sucked in a breath when Oren answered his phone.

"Baxter. Did you need anything?" he asked.

"Actually, I wanted to talk to you. You already know I made my decision, and I think it's time to act on it."

Oren hummed. "I'll accept your resignation, but I have an offer for you first."

Baxter frowned. This wasn't what was supposed to happen. "What offer?" he asked.

"Most of our team is relocating to the area where the pack is."

That wasn't what Baxter had expected. "Why?"

"The council recognizes the dragons are a threat and one we probably can't deal with on our own. They want us to work with the pack and any other supernatural group in the area, and I have to say I agree. We might not be used to fighting together, but in this case, we need to learn."

"And our team was chosen to do that?"

"I'm sure it has a lot to do with you and Robin already being with the pack. Robin isn't an enforcer anymore, so the council wants to ask him to be the liaison between the pack and us. You could do the same job but from our team."

Baxter didn't know what to say. He'd decided to leave the council, but he'd been worried about doing so when the dragons were still a problem. They'd have more resources if he stayed an enforcer, but he hadn't believed it would be possible to both be with Sloan and the pack and do his job. Now, Oren was offering a way around that, at least until the dragons were dealt with.

"Is everyone coming?" he asked.

Oren sighed. "Unfortunately, no. Ignatius is staying behind."

Baxter wasn't surprised. Ignatius had a partner and a young child, so it made sense he wouldn't want to relocate. Baxter was going to miss him, but he supposed they could still call each other. "What about the others?"

"They're all coming. Aubrey is, too, as well as Caley and Darren."

Those three, Baxter hadn't expected. "Why?"

"Darren is training to become a team member, and Caley wants to be there in case more bodies are discovered. As for Aubrey, well, he didn't want to be away from me for so long. He's not coming as a team member, but he'll be here."

"And how long is this going to last?"

"There's no way to know. We'll have to see what happens with the dragons. I suspect it'll take a while, though. Dragons are new enemies, and we're not sure how to deal with them."

Baxter knew that. He hadn't thought he'd continue being an enforcer, but now that he had the opportunity, he knew his answer. He wouldn't be an enforcer for the rest of his life, but he could stand doing it for a few more years until the dragons were dealt with. Hopefully, it wouldn't take that long, although considering dragons were immortal and rich, he suspected it wouldn't be easy. Thankfully, they had allies, people they'd never expected to work with. There was the pack, of course, but also Arlen and Merrick.

He looked at Sloan, trying to understand what the man he loved thought about this. Sloan shrugged, then leaned closer to whisper, "It's your decision. I'll stand by you, whatever you do."

Of course he would. He'd stand by Baxter because he was Sloan, gentle, sweet, and strong. He was supportive, and he'd always be there for Baxter, whatever Baxter decided.

They'd fight this battle together. Then, when it was over, Baxter would finally leave the enforcers behind and settle in a more peaceful life with the pack and Sloan. In the meantime, he'd fight for them as an enforcer.

Whoever said that anything worth having was also worth fighting for was right.

ABOUT THE AUTHOR

Catherine is the creator of several series, most of them paranormal, including the Whitedell Pride Series and the Gillham Pack Series. While she graduated in translation, she decided to go the writer's way because it was more fun to create her own stories and characters.

She's been living in Italy for more than twenty years, but she's a daughter of the North—Belgium to be precise—and she misses it so much that she's already planning to move back.

She loves pizza—probably too much—her son, her pets, and of course, books. She sneaks some reading time into her schedule every time she has five minutes free from writing, demands from her various pets and son, and lastly, housework.

Connect with her:

lievens.catherine@gmail.com

BookBub: https://www.bookbub.com/authors/catherine-lievens
Website: https://authorcatherinelievens.com/
Facebook: https://www.facebook.com/catherine.lievens.9
Facebook Group: https://www.facebook.com/groups/411788002341528/
Twitter: https://twitter.com/authorCLievens
Newsletter: http://eepurl.com/c-uvKn

www.ingramcontent.com/pod-product-compliance
Lightning Source LLC
Chambersburg PA
CBHW060637130626
46555CB00002B/839